This steer was an
outlaw in his blood.

HERE HE CAME, Elsa and sisters, he circled the ring, in spite of my best efforts to stun him with some Dog Karate. I mean, he was big enough and mean enough to eat Dog Karate for breakfast, and he tried.

It was a sad spectacle and a dark time for our ranch. Slim climbed over the icy fence and I scrambled under it, and we watched while the demented steer slammed into the trailer gate and hit the portable pen in three places, then...

This was bad, so prepare yourself. The nutcase steer wasn't able to destroy the equipment, so he circled the pen and leaped into the air, straddled a panel (and bent it), and tumbled to the ground— outside the pen. There, he got back on his feet, made a razzoo at Snips, and raced off to the north...TOWARD DOWNTOWN TWITCHELL!

Oh no! That had been our worst nightmare from the very start of this mission, that we'd have livestock running through town.

The Frozen Rodeo

John R. Erickson

Illustrations by Gerald L. Holmes

Maverick Books, Inc.

MAVERICK BOOKS, INC.

Published by Maverick Books, Inc.

P.O. Box 549, Perryton, TX 79070

Phone: 806.435.7611

www.hankthecowdog.com

First published in the United States of America by Maverick Books, Inc. 2020.

1 3 5 7 9 10 8 6 4 2

Copyright © John R. Erickson, 2020

LIBRARY OF CONGRESS CONTROL NUMBER: 2019950012

978-1-59188-174-2 (paperback); 978-1-59188-274-9 (hardcover)

Hank the Cowdog® is a registered trademark of John R. Erickson.

Printed in the United States of America

Dedicated to Gerald L. Holmes
1940 - 2019

I join the Maverick Books family in mourning the loss of our dear friend Gerald Holmes, the artist who drew the illustrations for 74 Hank the Cowdog books and put faces on Hank, Drover, Sally May, Slim and all the other characters.

Gerald began illustrating my magazine articles in 1978 when he worked in a feedlot and I was working on a ranch. We had no money but had talent, energy, and big dreams, and we set out to do things that hadn't been done before.

We worked together for 41 years. I didn't tell him what to draw and he didn't tell me what to write. We never quarreled and he never missed a deadline.

Gerald took his art into homes and schools and hospitals, to cow camps and deer blinds and drilling rigs. He did with art what I hoped to do with the written word: deliver the blessing of innocent laughter.

And he did it so well! He illuminated the imaginations of millions of children and there is no way to calculate how many of them drew their first picture, imitating Gerald's Hank or Drover.

We mourn the loss of this gentle, humble man and celebrate the joy he brought into the world. Our prayers go out to his wife Carol and sons, Heath and Chris.

John and Kris Erickson & Family
Gary and Kim Rinker & Family
Trev Tevis
Nikki Earley
Janee McCartor

CONTENTS

CHAPTER ONE

A Wasp Crisis

It's me again, Hank the Cowdog. The mystery began in the spring, as I recall, a few weeks after Christmas. Wait. Christmas comes in the month of December, and the last time I checked, December falls in the winter, not the spring.

Hencely, the mystery couldn't have begun in the spring, so disregard the previous message. The mystery began in the wintertime, January, yes of course, when Slim and I found ourselves roping cattle in downtown Twitchell during an ice storm.

Oops, you're not supposed to know about that because it comes later in the story. See, what comes later can't come sooner, so let's be very quiet about this and not blab it around, okay? We won't

1

tell anyone that Miss Viola was there and so were the police. Oh, and the dogcatcher. Shhhh.

Now let's get to the business of the fire. It was in the winter, the very worst time for your house to burn down. I was the one who first saw the flames and turned in the alarm, so I know what I'm talking about. I mean, I was inside the house.

It was a very tense and scary situation, and already I'm wondering if we should go on with the story. You know how I am about the little children: give 'em a few thrills and let 'em have fun, but don't load 'em down with the scariest parts of my work.

Hey, a dog in my position is trained to cope with the scary stuff—the crinimal investigations, the constant battle with the Charlies, the Red Alert emergencies, and fires of all kinds—but the kids don't have that kind of preparation.

What do you think? Should we plunge into the story or call it quits and go do something else?

I figured that's what you'd say. Okay, you'd better grab hold of something stout and hang on. Here we go.

We've already decided that it happened in the wintertime. Drover and I had pretty muchly moved our base of operations from the gas tanks down to Slim Chance's shack, two miles east of ranch headquarters.

Why? Because Slim was a bachelor cowboy who allowed the Elite Troops of the Security Division to stay inside the house on cold winter nights, and that was a big deal. He had a nice wood-burning stove in the living room and we made our camp on the floor, near the stove. His carpet was as thin as the seat of his pants, but all in all, it was a great place to be on a cold winter night.

We had made it through the deep dark of the night with no emergency calls to interrupt our sleep. We were safe, warm, and comfortable on the floor. I don't recall what woke me up...wait, yes I do, a yellow jacket wasp dropped from the ceiling and landed on my head.

We don't expect wasps to fall on our heads in January. In a normal year, we don't even see a wasp in January. Why? I'm not sure. Most usually they show up in the spring, hang around all summer, and make a nuisance of themselves in the fall, and they're gone by the time snow arrives.

Maybe they fly south with the birds. Maybe they buzz themselves to death in the fall, and that's why you find all those crunchy dead ones around window sills. But the point is that we never see them in January, but that particular January, we were seeing plenty of them. They

3

were still lurking around, and nobody on my ranch was glad about it, especially me.

Do we have time for this? I mean, talking about yellow jacket wasps seems a waste of time, especially when we have classified information that our house was fixing to burn down around our heads. On the other hand, wasps are a pretty serious threat to public safety, so maybe we should say a few more words about them.

The main point here is that your average wasp is armed and dangerous. He carries a loaded stinger on the end of his tail and has no respect for the rights of people or dogs. One day a wasp crawled into Slim's boot and guess what happened when he stuck his foot inside.

Wow, it sounded like the blast of a bull moose, scared me and Drover out of three months' growth. He got over it, Slim did, but it sure darkened his mood for the rest of the morning, and he started checking his boots for booby-traps.

Oh, and he stopped walking around the house in his bare feet. Can you guess why? Because one night, right before supper, he stepped on a wasp and got knifed, so he dug out his old pair of sheepskin house slippers. He started wearing them around the house, don't you see, and when he spotted a yellow jacket creeping around on the floor, he made a special effort to smash it.

Those slippers were patched with duct tape because…well, some unknown villain had chewed them up, but we don't need to probe any deeper into that chapter of our lives. See, we never caught the Slipper Shredder, but guess who got blamed. Not Drover, a prime suspect in the case, and not Sally May's rotten little cat, not the coyote brothers or Eddy the Rac.

Me. I got blamed! No kidding, and I was the Lead Investigator on the case. Outrageous!

Anyway, how did we get on the subject of slipskin sheepers? I don't know, but before we leave that subject, let me whisper a Deep Dark Secret: Dogs who have dabbled in the sheepskin business will tell you…

Maybe we'd better skip the rest of this. I don't think it would do either of us any good.

The main point here is that I know almost nothing about the sleepskin shippers, and to this very day, the case remains unsolved.

Now, where were we? Oh yes, the Wasp Crisis. I was in the midst of a peaceful sleep, on the floor of Slim's bachelor shack, only moments before the place went up in flames, when something landed on my right ear and tripped an alarm in Data Control.

Naturally I tried to ignore it. Who wants to be disturbed in the middle of a peaceful sleep? Not me, but our sensors were picking up tiny signals suggesting that something was walking around up there. In other words, this wasn't a piece of plaster that had fallen from the ceiling. Plaster fragments don't have legs.

I punched in the commands for Ear Flick— twice, three times. No luck there. The motion sensors were still picking up creepy little signals on one of my ears and DC (that's our code for Data Control) kicked on the General Alarm.

Gongs gonged and lights flashed, and I found myself standing on the bridge, shouting into a microphone. "All hands on deck! Bring sidearms and sandwiches, we've got pork chops creeping through the catnip! Approach and capture! Repeat: capture the roaches, this is not a drill!"

Things were a little foggy at that point, I mean we had sailors shouting and gongs blaring, very confusing, but someone must have activated the circuit for Hind Leg Scratch. My right hind leg swung into action and began a Hacking Procedure on the starboard ear, which resulted in...well, a sharp stinging sensation.

OWWWWW!

It stung like crazy. We had taken a direct hit

from a missile or a torpedo, right in the...

HUH?

Okay, the stupid wasp had dropped from the ceiling and landed on my ear, and when that happens, the last thing you want to do is rough him up with a burst of scratching. Do you know why? Because you probably won't kill the little heathen, and he will drill you with his poison stinger.

That's obvious when you're wide awake, but when you explode out of a deep sleep, it's not so obvious, and yes, I followed the wrong procedure and got drilled, and the saddest part was that I didn't even bag the wasp. I heard the buzz of his wings as he flew off to torment someone else.

Trembling with righteous anger, I blinked my eyes and glanced around. Okay, it appeared that I was in Slim's living room, and there was a corpse on the floor beside me. Wait, that might have been Drover and he might have been merely conked out asleep. That was good news and I was about to shut everything down, when I noticed...

Good grief, the inside of the house was RED, and we're not talking about slightly red. This was a bright, fiery red, and that's when I was smoten by the awful reality.

OUR HOUSE WAS BURNING DOWN!!

CHAPTER TWO

The House Is On Fire!

Hold up, there's something we need to discuss. Is *smoten* the right word for this particular situation, or should it be *smitten*?

You know how I am about getting the right word for every situation. If we don't set a good example for the kids, the next thing you know, they'll be talking and acting like monkeys. They'll start eating bananas and tossing all their peelings on the floor. Their ears will sprout hair and they'll start scratching their armpits.

Is that the kind of behavior we want to see in the little children? Is that the kind of world we want to leave for our granddogs? Absolutely not, and it all starts right here, in the way we use language. Don't forget: Without words, we'd all

9

be speechless.

A lot of mutts don't care and wouldn't take the time to get it right. You know who cares? Cowdogs. We have to be just a little bit special, so let's stop right here and take the time to get it right.

Write-wrote-written

Kite-coat-kitten

Bite-boat-bitten

Smite-smote-smitten

Okay, there we are, that's the answer. It should be *smitten*, not written, kitten, mitten, or bitten. The next time you see a monkey, tell him to shape up and stop using trashy language. What belongs in the trash are banana peelings and peanut shells.

Sorry, I didn't mean to get carried away, but somebody has to take a stand on these issues.

Where were we? I have no idea. It was something important, but it seems to have vanished in a fog. Maybe that was it, fog. We'd had a few foggy mornings after Christmas, and a dog can get lost in a fog. So can a frog.

I'm just killing time, waiting for something to click.

This is so annoying. To be honest, it drives me nuts. In my line of work, I have to stay focused and organized. Nobody expects much out of

Drover. He can fill his mind with all kinds of nonsense, but the Head of Ranch Security has to...

Wait, hold everything, I've got it! THE HOUSE WAS ON FIRE! How could you have forgotten that? You know what? You need to start paying attention!

Okay, now we're rolling. I was inside Slim's house, remember? I'd been assaulted by a wasp and was wide awake, and when I glanced around, I noticed that the room inside of which I was whiching had turned a bright shade of red, fiery red.

And fellers, I knew we were in deep trouble.

I reached for the microphone of my mind and hit the button for 911 Alert. "May we have your attention please? This is the Special Crimes Division. We have fire in the hole! Fire in the house! You're about to be barbecued alive, but please don't panic!"

The alarm had a magical effect on Drover. I mean, the runt came flying out of a brick-like sleep, jumped three feet in the air and seemed to be swimming, then hit the ground and began running in circles. "Help, murder, mayday, there's a hole in the fire!"

"Calm down, soldier, and stand by for orders! Proceed to your duty station and begin barking the alarm. We must evacuate the house and Slim must be warned!"

"Forget, that, I'm out of here!"

"Drover, hold your duty station and..."

He went streaking down the hall toward the bedroom, screeching, "Red, red, everything's red! Under the bed or we'll all be dead!"

You know, panic can be contagious. I mean, the house was filling with smoke and fire, flaming rafters were falling all around us, and Drover was racing down the hall, screeching insane poetry about being fried alive.

So, yes, I lost all discipline and went racing down the hall behind him. He dived under Slim's bed and a moment later, I was right beside him. Even inside the bunker, everything was red, and I won't deny that we were terrified.

It's kind of mysterious that in such an extreme emergency situation, Drover began speaking in rhymes, isn't it? I can't explain it.

But there we were, huddled under the bed. I had to bring some order into the chaos. "All right, men, call in your damage reports. Has anyone suffered burns?"

"No burns, but I can't breathe!"

"Why can't you breathe?"

"All the smoke makes me choke."

"Oh yes, the smoke is terrible. Install smoke

12

filters at once."

"I don't have any."

"Neither do I, so we'll have to breathe through our noses."

"Yeah, bud by doze is stobbed ubb."

"What?"

"By doze. Id's stobbed ubb. I bust be allergig to sboge."

"Drover, what language are you speaking?"

"I'b dot sure, but I gant breathe through by doze."

"You can't breathe through your toes?"

"Doe, by doze!"

"Doe, ray, me? Are you trying to sing?"

"You dever lizzen!"

"A better lizard? What are you talking about? Wait, let's try facial expressions. Give me some kind of clue." I studied his face. "Okay, I'm getting it now. Your eyes are crossed. You saw a lizard and you crossed your eyes and now they're hung in the crossed position?"

"Doe, doe!"

"Well, if I'm a dodo, what are you? You can't even talk straight."

"Helb!"

"Listen, pal, it's too late for me to give you speaking lessons. The house is on fire and..." I sniffed the air and suddenly realized.... "Drover,

I just noticed something odd."

"Whud?"

"The house is on fire but there's no smoke."

"There's nod?"

"No. It must be some kind of smokeless fire."

"I'll be derned. I thought I couldn't breathe because of all the smoke."

"You couldn't breathe because your eyes were crossed. Stop crossing your eyes and let's bark the alarm. We've got to get Slim out of bed. Come on, son, and load up your biggest barks!"

I crawled out from under the bed and was confronted by the terrible redness of the fire. Oh, you should have seen it! Once out in the open, I loaded up Number Three Warning Barks and began blasting away. Drover joined me and added a few squeaks, and we began pumping them out, bark after bark, blast upon blast.

As you know, getting Slim out of his bed is always a challenge. I mean, the guy is a hard-head. But even Slim was no match for our barrage of barking. We pumped 'em out, until at last he sat up and...yipes, was that Slim or some kind of monster? I mean, the face looked like something you might see on a gut wagon.

But then he spoke...roared, actually...he roared, "Hush up! Knock off the dadgum barking!"

He blinked his eyes and glanced around. "Good honk, everything's red!"

Oh good, it was Slim after all, and he was exactly right. DUH. Everything was red because *the house was on fire*, and if he didn't pry himself out of that bed, we were all going to get barbecued!

He kicked off his blankets, dived out of bed, and trotted down the hall in his Winter Sleep Outfit: one-piece red long-john underwear, bare feet, and a buzzard's nest of hair. Drover and I were right behind him, scared out of our wits. He ran to the door, threw it open, and stared at the... well, at the sky, I suppose, which appeared to be ablaze with fiery red and orange colors.

Good grief, the fire was outside too! In other words, the whole world was on fire, not just the house! And when the whole world is on fire, where does a dog go to hide?

Hey, I tried to warn you that this was going to be a spooky story, but did you listen? Oh no, you thought you were old enough and tough enough to handle anything that came along. Now look at the mess we're in!

So what do we do now? I can tell you what Drover did. His eyes almost bugged out of his head. He let out a squeak, "Oh my gosh!", and fainted right there on the floor, and we're talking

about going down like a pine tree.   BAM!

That left me and Slim, staring at the flaming sky—and he was still in his underwear! How do you suppose that made me feel? The guy in charge, the guy whose house was about to burn down, was running around in underwear that was the same color as the inferno outside, RED!

Wait, was that some kind of clue? It sounds kind of mysterious, red underwear and red sky. Maybe not.

Even so, things were looking bad, maybe even hopeless. I can't guarantee that there's any way out of this deal, but if you want to stick with me, we'll find out what happened—good, bad, or awful—in the next chapter.

If you can't hang on, I understand. I don't want to hang on either, but I've got no choice. Wish me luck.

CHAPTER THREE

Smoke, Flames, Awful!

~~~~~~

Are you still with me? Good, I wasn't sure which way it would go, but I'm glad you stuck with me. It's pretty scary when the whole world is on fire, when one of your companions has fainted like spilled milk on the floor and the other is running around in his underwear.

Okay, let's take a deep breath and try to get organized. Maybe we can find a way out.

Let's start with a clue that you might have missed. Remember that cloud of choking smoke inside the house, the same smoke that set off Drover's allergies and caused him to speak in an unknown language?

Here's the clue: THERE WASN'T ANY SMOKE! I had made this discovery when Drover and I

18

were hiding in the bunker, and I said that we seemed to be involved in some kind of mysterious "smokeless fire." Remember that? When I made the comment, Drover's allergies suddenly vanished and he began speaking in Normal Bow Wow.

Do you see what this means? Number One, Drover's allergy attack was a bogus event, which, Number Two, confirmed something we have known for years, that Drover is a notorious hypocardiac.

You can't trust the little mutt when he goes into his sneezing fits and starts talking about how his "doze is stobbed ub." At least half the time, he's making it up.

Oh brother. But there was a third clue in this Mystery of The Whole World On Fire, and it came from the guy who was running around the house in his red long-john underwear: Slim Chance.

Let's reset the stage. Slim opened the front door and was looking outside at the eastern horizon...or was it the western horizon? No, it had to be eastern because this was morning and the sun comes up in the east, right? Okay, we're making progress.

So Slim was looking at the flaming sky. Drover fainted and fell on the floor. I was wondering how a dog escapes from a fire that is engulferating the entire world, and waiting for Slim to come up with some kind of plan to save us.

At that very tense and scary moment, Slim's eyes grew wide and he said something that blew the case wide open, and this became the crucial Third Clue. He said, and this is a direct quote, he said, "Man alive, I've never seen such a red sunrise!"

WHAT!

Sunrise?

Okay, we're going to call off the Code Three and try to relax a little bit. Ha ha. Do you get it now? Whew! Boy, you talk about getting scared out of six months' growth!

Let's take it a step at a time. Remember all that red color inside the house? You thought the house was on fire and you thought burning rafters were falling around our ears. Hey, even I was fooled for a minute or two, and that's why I raced down the hallway and took cover in the bunker. But it didn't take me long to figure out...

Okay, let's try to be honest here. Being honest isn't always fun, but it's always right. The truth, the painful truth, is that I got sandbagged, completely fooled by the bright red sunrise, but let me hasten to point out that any dog would have been fooled. Hey, when you wake up and the whole house is red, you naturally think it's on fire.

Furthermore, Drover was no help at all. In fact, he got fooled ten times worse than I did, and don't forget that he was choking on smoke that *didn't exist*. That gives you some idea of what I have to put up with in this job. My assistant is a ninny and a harpofoliac.

Let me point out another important piece of evidence: I was operating under the influence of wasp poison. That was a huge factor in the overall so-forth of this case, because wasp poison is very toxic, right? And it stings *like fire*, right?

There you are, that explains everything. Any dog who'd been stung by a wasp and saw red inside the house would have thought that the house was burning down.

And don't forget that Slim had never seen such a bright red sunrise in his whole life. Was it my fault that the brightest, reddest sunrise in history happened on my watch? No sir. They try to blame the dogs for everything that goes wrong on this outfit, but they can't blame us for the sunrise.

Anyway, we made it through a very scary situation and I'm glad you stuck with me. I really appreciate your help.

Where were we? Oh yes, Slim was standing in the screen door, admiring the sunrise that had turned the clouds, the horizon, and the inside of our house a bright shade of red.

"You know, my ma used to say, 'Red sky at morning, sailor take warning. Red sky at night, sailor's delight.' Makes me wonder if our weather is fixing to change." He was quiet for a moment. "Boy, I wish I had a camera. You know, I used to have one. Maybe I can find it, but I'd better hurry. Out of the way, dogs!"

Huh? Suddenly and without warning, he changed from being a slow-walking, slow-talking bachelor cowboy, into a stampeding buffalo. What was I supposed to do? In the morning, he usually moves around like a man under water. I had never seen him sprinting around the house at that time of day. I was so shocked, I just sat there and, well, he ran over me…and tripped.

He kept his feet for a few thundering steps, then plowed into that little table beside his sitting chair. Plowing the table wasn't a big deal, I mean, it was stout enough to take some bumping around, but there was a lamp sitting on it, the antique lamp he had inherited from Aunt Olive, as I recall. It had a big shade and a light bulb, and it was mostly made of some kind of breakable material—porcelain or china, the stuff plates are made of, and it had flowers painted on it.

Why would anyone make a lamp out of

breakable material? And why did Slim keep it in his shack? Beats me. If a bachelor cowboy is going to keep a lamp in his house, it ought to be made of rebar and cement, something tasteless and ugly that won't break.

And the painted flowers were a total waste. Slim was flower-blind. He wouldn't notice a flower unless it jumped out and bit him.

Anyway, he plowed into the table and the lamp went crashing to the floor. It sounded bad and it didn't look so pretty either—we're talking about things broken into little pieces—and, naturally, I felt terrible. After all, I had played a small but tiny part in the tragedy.

I rushed to his side and gave him a juicy, healing lick on the cheek. Actually, I aimed for his cheek but got his nose. He must have moved his head at the last second, but nose-licks can deliver almost as much emotional punch as a cheek-lick, and I gave him a big, juicy nose-lick with all my heart and soil.

He pushed me away and yelled, "Now look what you've done! Get out of my way!" He pushed himself up to his feet and limped to the closet.

Obviously, my lick had been wasted. And notice who got blamed for the busted lamp. ME.

He jerked open the closet door and, well, that

was a mistake too. I could have told him, but he didn't ask and he never listens anyway. The closet was crammed with all kinds of stuff: boots, coats, vests, a yellow slicker, chaps, gloves, straw hats, felt hats, and three rolls of toilet paper. It had all been jammed inside and when he opened the door, some of it—a lot of it—spilled out into the room.

What didn't come out in the avalanche remained inside the closet, which was so dark he would never find the camera. I mean, that was the whole purpose of this fiasco, wasn't it? He was looking for a camera?

Trying to help, I barked a message: "If you want to find the camera, you'd better get a flashlight."

He turned to me with bared fangs and snarled, "Quit barking!" Then he stomped into the kitchen and began plundering drawers, in search of a flashlight.

Gee, what a grouch. How can a dog help his people if he can't bark? I mean, that's what we do, we *bark* our messages. What did he expect me to do, oink or meow my advice? As I've said before, in many ways, this is a lousy job.

Phooey on him. I had better things to do anyway, because I noticed that the King of

Slackers had recovered from his fainting spell and was back on his feet. In fact, he was standing over one of the rolls of toilet paper and pointing it with his nose, like a bird dog pointing quail.

When I marched over to him, he gave me a silly grin. "Oh, hi. I guess the house wasn't on fire."

"That's correct, but you fainted anyway."

"Yeah, you got me all scared, but it was just the sunrise that made everything look red."

"Correct again. We had no fire and there wasn't even a whiff of smoke in the house, so how do you explain your weird behavior?"

"Which weird behavior?"

"You went into a spasm of sneezing and claimed that you were choking to death on the smoke."

His grin widened. "Oh yeah, that was pretty weird, bud subbtibes by doze geds stobbed ub."

"It's worse than weird. It's abnormal. What are you doing?"

"When?"

"Right now, this very instant."

"Oh. Look what I found."

"It's a roll of toilet paper. So what?"

"Watch this." He nudged the roll with his nose. It moved forward, leaving a path of paper behind it. "It's kind of neat."

"It's kind of neat, but it's not something a dog

should be...you pushed it with your nose?"

"Yeah, it was easy. Want me to show you?"

"That won't be necessary. In fact, step aside and I'll show you a thing or two. Pay attention."

"Yeah, but..."

"Move."

And with that, I gave the runt a lesson in Paper Unrolleration.

CHAPTER FOUR

Decorating
Slim's House

I must give Drover credit for discovering this new amusement, and I'll admit that I'd never done it before, or had even thought about doing it. I mean, viewed from a certain angle, you might be tempted to say that it was a little ridiculous—a dog pushing a roll of paper around with his nose.

But right away, I sensed that...how can I say this? I was seized by a feeling that this little exercise could transfume into something...well, artistic, something that expressed a dog's Inner Dogness. Something with Meaning.

Most of your ordinary mutts know nothing about this kind of thing, I mean, in an average day, they spend their time sleeping, scratching fleas, and figuring out new ways to say, "Duhhhh."

But those of us who live on top of the mountaintop have a broader, deeper view of things. We're aware of higher emotions that *can't* be expressed through barks or saying "duh."

It's a powerful desire to make the world just a little nicer than it was before, through a Work of Art.

And somehow, in a flash of insight, that's what I saw in this exercise—an opportunity to reveal a new form of beauty that was hidden inside the Paper Roll of Life. It was right there in front of me, like a flower that hadn't bloomed. All I had to do was make it happen.

I cleared Mister Squeakbox out of the way, loosened up the muscles in my enormous shoulders, took a semi-crouched position in front of the paper roll, and lined up my nose. When everything was set and ready, I crept forward and gave it a nudge. It moved forward, leaving a perfect trail of white bunting material.

"Look at that, son. Is that impressive or what?"

"Yeah, that's what I was doing."

"That's NOT what you were doing. You were just pushing and shoving without any kind of thought or pattern. It was a careless amusement. This is something entirely different."

"Yeah, but…"

"Drover, instead of arguing, why don't you pay

attention? You might actually learn something."

"It kind of hurts my feelings."

"You'll get over it."

I returned to my work, lined up my nose, and gave the paper another nudge, this time with more punch. The roll leaped forward, leaving a perfect little highway of white paper in its wake. In a rush of inspiration, I did it again, only this time I moved beyond the Nudge Procedure and gave it a pretty solid push with an upward thrust of my nose.

Amazing! It rolled into the hallway, while I maintained a disciplined position right behind it. See, in this kind of exercise, the disciplined position is everything. You have to maintain your spacing, don't you know, so that when the roll slows down, you're right there to keep it moving.

Hey, I was really on a roll now!

A little humor there, did you get it? I was ON A ROLL, rolling a roll of paper down the hall. Ha ha.

Anyway, things were turning out great and I had gotten the technique down to a fine art. Halfway down the hall, I picked up speed, batted and chased the roll to the end of the hallway, into Slim's bedroom, and under his bed.

At that point, things got more complicated. In the confined space beneath the bed, I found it

impossible to keep up the momentum of the momentum. The roll stopped unrolling, in other words, so I had to shift tactics. With a mighty upward thrust of the nose, I sent it flying out from beneath the bed, then scrambled out and.... BONK...made a slight miscalculation about the height of the stupid bed, but it was only a temporary setback.

Ouch.

Once I'd cleared the bed, I resumed the Chasing Position and went flying down the hallway and back into the living room. I mean, it was really something to see. You've seen hockey players racing across the ice in pursuit of the muck? Same deal. I wasn't wearing skates or swinging a hockey pick, but, fellers, this was pockery in motion, a dog on a mission to decorate the world with an artful expression of Papericity!

Hey, I was bringing new forms of beauty into the drab dungeon of Slim's shack.

Back in the living room, I had to shut down the whole procedure because, well, I ran out of paper. I mean, the roll just vanished and became an empty tube of cardboard, which was a bummer. I was just hitting my stride with this deal.

At that point, I noticed a strange man standing in front of the closet, shining a flashlight inside and pawing through things on the shelf. Good grief, was this a burglar who had broken into the house whilst I'd been occupied with Arts and Crafts?

I had never seen this guy before, and he sure as thunder had no business rummaging around in Slim's closet!

The hair along my backbone sprang upward and I began loading up some big-time Stop the Intruder Barks. If those barks didn't do the job, I might have to launch a Fang Missile and put a big bite right in the middle of his...

Wait, hold everything. He was wearing red long-john underwear. Do you remember...ha ha, never mind, it was only Slim. I guess he was looking for his camera. Ha ha.

Okay, the Take-Away Point here is that the Head of Ranch Security is never off duty. We never get time off or a vacation. Our work never ends, and we have to remain vinegar at all times.

Virulent

Vigital.

Vegetable.

Digital.

Phooey. We have to remain alert at all times, and I can tell you from hard experience that it isn't easy, because Slim Chance is such a goof-off, we never know when he's really in danger and when he's just pulling another childish prank on the dogs. This time, he wasn't.

Vigilant. That's the word. We have to remain *vegetable* at all times.

Where were we? Oh yes, Slim was looking for the camera so that he could, I don't know, take a picture of something. The sunrise, the brilliant red sunrise.

Now we're cooking. He actually found the camera in the mess of the closet, with the help of a flashlight. He held the camera close to his face and heaved a sigh. "By grabs, it even has film!"

He rushed to the door, flung it open...wait, is it flung or flang? It doesn't matter, he flang open the door, stepped out on the porch in his bare feet, brought the camera up to his eye, and... oops, the sunrise that would have made such a beautiful picture had melted away, leaving nothing but a gray sky with gray clouds.

His shoulders slumped and I heard him grumble, "Boy, the bus don't wait long around here."

He came back inside the house and closed the door. At that point, his eyes began moving around the room. Ah, good, he was finally noticing my Work: a hundred feet of white bunting that decorated his house in a fresh, artistic manner it had never known before.

But then...

Yipes, his face began to harden, I mean, it looked like the trunk of a hackberry tree: rough, wrinkled, ugly. No, it was worse than that. Remember that sometimes in the morning, when his hair is in shambles, he begins to look like a vampire? Well, that Vampire Look was coming back, and all at once, I...I lost confidence that the man before me was really Slim Chance.

Don't laugh. If you've never been a dog, if you've never been involved in life and death struggles with vampires and Charlie Monsters, you just don't know how strange this world can be. I mean, things never stay the same. Our enemies will show up in a clever disguise (a bachelor cowboy), then change into another (a burglar), and before you know it, they've change into a third disguise (a vampire).

We know what they're doing. They're trying to confuse the dogs, and I'm sad to report that sometimes it works. We try to adjust our systems and tactics, but it's impossible to beat them at their own game all the time. Once in a while, they change costumes so fast, they slip through our security net, and then we've got a problem that goes all the way to top management.

And let me tell you, our toughest decisions

come at us at seventy miles an hour. I mean, we're standing in the middle of the highway, blinded by headlights, and we have about two seconds to choose from a narrow menu of options: run, fight, or bark.

That's where we were on this deal, and I had to make a decision, fast. I hit the button for Option Three and began blasting out some big ones, the kind of barks that produce such a powerful recoil, a dog bounces backward on every...

"Hush!"

...bark. Okay, maybe it was Slim again, but how's a dog supposed to know?

He pointed a bony finger at the strips of bunting paperwork, and spoke in a voice that sounded like a hacksaw cutting pipe. "Did you do that?"

Who? I glanced around. Where was Drover? He had vanished, the little...wait, there he was, cowering beneath the coffee table, but Slim wasn't looking for Drover. His eyes came at me like bullets.

"Bird brain! First you wreck the lamp, then you toilet-paper my house! Out! Scat!"

He flang open the door again and pointed, well, outside, it seemed, and maybe he wanted me to leave.

Fine, I could leave.

I shifted my ears and tail into the Rebuked Display and went slinking toward the door. I had a feeling that, as I slank past him, he would boot me in the tail with his foot, and he did.

It didn't hurt all that much (he was barefooted), but it seemed undignified. Our people just don't understand how hard it is to be a dog.

Moments later, the door opened again and Drover came flying out. Mister Grumpy McGrumble had pitched him out, and there we were on the porch of the house that didn't burn down, two loyal dogs who had been tricked, rebuked and rejected.

The runt skidded to a stop, collapsed on the porch, and began bawling. "He threw me out of the house and I didn't do anything wrong! I was just tying to stay out of the way. It breaks my heart!"

Would I go to the trouble of comforting him in his time of need? Sure. His little heart was broken and he needed a friend. I made my way over to the spot where he was kicking all four legs, and prepared for the ordeal of listening to him moan and whine.

CHAPTER FIVE

Words of Comfort

I sat down beside his potsrate body and gave him several fatherly pats on the rib cage. "There, there."

He stopped kicking his legs and stared at me through tear-soaked eyes. "What?"

"I said, 'There, there.'"

"What's that supposed to mean?"

"Well, it means...it's a way of expressing sympathy."

"There, there?"

"Yes, exactly. Those two words are filled with sympathy."

"Yeah, but it was only one word and you said it twice."

"Drover, I'm aware of that. When you repeat

the word, somehow it picks up an extra load of sympathy."

"It doesn't sound very sympathetic to me."

"Well, maybe you're too picky for your own good. Look, I'm the one who came over here to show concern, and I can choose my own words. Those were the words that came from my heart."

"Yeah, but they don't mean anything. You could have said, 'There, there, it's just not fair.' That would have meant something, and it even rhymes."

"Yes, or I could have said, 'There, there, I just don't care.' That rhymes too."

His chin trembled. "I'm going to cry."

"Don't cry! It grates on my nerves."

"If it's so great, why can't I do it?"

I stared into the vast emptiness of his eyeballs. "Are you trying to be funny?"

"Doe, I'b dod."

"What?"

"It's by allergies. Whid I gry, they stard ag-ding ub."

"That's my whole point. Stop crying."

"Well, I guess I cad dry." He sniffled and wiped his eyes. "There, does this sound better?"

"Much better. See, when you talk with your nose stopped up, it makes you sound like a goofball."

"Sorry."

"You're welcome. Now, what were we talking about?"

"You got me in trouble—again. I didn't do anything wrong, but Slim yelled at me and threw me out of the house."

"And you're blaming me for that?"

"Well, you woke everybody up and said the house was on fire."

"Drover, everything had turned red. I was just trying to do my job. But if it will make you feel better, I'll admit that I was misquoted. Does that help?"

"No, 'cause then you stole the toilet paper."

I groaned. "I did not *steal* the toilet paper, and it wasn't yours to start with. I was merely trying to teach you a new and exciting way of decorating a house, but were you grateful? Oh no. And now you're trying to blame me for your broken heart."

"Yeah, it's smashed, and I need to cry."

"You will NOT cry. Be strong and brave. Shake it off."

"Well, okay." He rose to his feet and shook his entire body, from nose to stub tail. It released a blizzard of white hairs into the atmosphere, and he grinned. "You know, I think that helped. I'm feeling better."

"Good, good. We've made some progress. Now let's see if we can build on it."

"Gosh, how do we do that?"

"First, we will bring this ridiculous conversation to an end. No more whining or sniffling. No more allergy attacks, and no more blaming me for all your problems."

"Yeah, but…"

"Second, we're going to sing a song about unrolling the toilet paper."

"That's weird."

"I beg your pardon?"

"I said, what if we don't know the song?"

I moved my nose closer to his face. "Drover, nobody knows the song. We'll compose it on the spot. We'll write it from scratch." Suddenly, he sat down and began hacking at his ear with a hind paw. "Why are you doing that?"

"I don't know. All at once, I had to scratch."

"Scratch on your own time. We're fixing to burst into song. We'll be doing it in the key of G-Whiz. Our starting note will be K-Sharp."

"BK-Sharp?"

"K-Sharp."

"Okay."

"Not O-K. K-Sharp!"

"You don't need to screech."

"And you don't need to scratch! Get the note right. What's wrong with you?"

"I'm all confused."

I glanced around and blinked my eyes. "You know what? I'm a little confused myself. Do you suppose it's just us? I mean, let's face it. If someone were listening, he might think that we're a couple of morons."

"That's hard to believe."

"I know it sounds crazy, but...never mind. Let's knock out the song."

Whew! You see what I have to put up with around here? Carrying on a conversation with Drover is exhausting, and sometimes I feel that I'm trying to walk through a vat of glue. Never mind, let's do the song. Here we go.

Decorating Slim's House

Hank
That toilet paper caper really flopped.
Hey, I pushed the roll around until I dropped.
I started out with expectation
That this bit of decoration
Would improve the looks of Slim's ugly shack.

I guess I should have known he wouldn't
    see the point
Of me trying to add some color to his joint.
The problem was, he has no taste,
And all my efforts went to waste.
I wonder why a dog should even care.

Drover
The idea of rolling paper came from me.
It wasn't yours and you borrowed it for free.
You butted in and then you rolled it,
But the truth is that you stole it.
I couldn't believe you did that to a friend.

I had to watch you while you had all the fun,
Chasing paper through the house at a run.
But it turned out not so bad,
You made a mess and Slim got mad.
And all that I can say is "Tee hee hee!"

Hank
Drover...sigh.
It's so sad to see you showing no respect
For your leader who got caught up in a wreck.
I was trying my very hardest
To give expression like an artist,
And I still say the result was pretty neat.

So, oh well, I got in trouble, that's not new.
But Drover, don't forget that so did you!
Even though you tried to hide,
You still got blamed and tossed outside,
And here we are together, Tee hee hee.

Drover
Yeah, even though I tried to hide,
I still got blamed and tossed outside.
It isn't fair and I think I'm going to cry!

Well, that was our song. What do you think? It wasn't the best thing we'd ever done, but it wasn't so bad either. Actually, I thought it was pretty cute, and I liked the part about Drover getting into trouble. Hee hee.

But I could see that it was about to set him off on another round of boo-hooing. All the symptoms were there: the down-turned mouth, the quivering lip, and big tears shining in the corners of his eyes. I searched my memory for words of comfort that might halt the slide of his tears: what could I say to make the little guy feel better?

And you know what? As if by magic, the words popped into my mind, and maybe they

were just the right ones for this moment. I rushed over to him, patted him on the back, and said, "There, there."

He stared at me for a long moment. "You already said that."

"I did?"

"Yeah, and it sounded dumb. We even talked about it."

"Hmm. You know, you could be right." I paced a few steps away. "Drover, sometimes the deeper layers of meaning don't appear at first. We have to repeat our words repeat our words and hear them again again."

"You mean..."

"Yes. Let's try it again, but this time I'll put more feeling into it." I turned and faced him and delivered the message again: "There...there!"

He blinked and rolled his eyes around. "Try it one more time."

I filled my chest with fresh carbon diego and leaned toward him. "There...THERE!"

The corners of his mouth began bending upward into a smile, and I seemed to detect a... well, a look of tranquittery in his eyes. And he said—this is a direct quote—he said, "I'll be derned. Why didn't you say that in the first place?"

The question hung in the air as we gazed into each others' eyes. In that long, throbbing silence, I began to realize...I began to understand that Drover was one of the weirdest little mutts I'd ever met, and that most of what we'd been talking about over the past fifteen minutes *made no sense*—I mean, ZERO.

Oh well, he wasn't sobbing his life away and seemed to be feeling better. In fact, within seconds, he was hopping around on the porch and had returned to the happy little guy we'd always known.

Wow. Sometimes I wonder...never mind.

CHAPTER SIX

Uh Oh, the Boss
Shows Up

You know what? Drover had raised a pretty interesting question: What was so comforting about a dog saying, "There, there"? Viewed from a certain angle, it sounded, well, empty, but that's all the time we can spend on Words of Comfort.

If you found parts of the last chapter confusing, don't worry about it. Try to keep in mind a nugget of Cowdog Wisdom: The mind of a dog is an awesome thing, but the fact that it's awesome doesn't mean that we can always understand what it's doing.

So there we were on Slim's porch. Drover and I had been ejected from the house on trumped-up charges. We had written and performed a pretty crackerjack song, and I had helped Drover through a difficult time in his little life.

Things were looking better for us, but a cloud still hung over our world. Slim. The last time we'd seen him, he had been in a dark, foul mood. Angry. His morning hadn't started well, shall we say, and he had blamed it on his loyal dogs.

No dog on this ranch could have been surprised. Getting tagged for everything that had ever gone wrong in the world was just part of a normal day around here.

Okay, in the interest of fairness, I have to admit that the Toilet Paper Caper might have gone over the line just a wee bit. Even though I had gone into the procedure with the best of intentions, a neutral observer might have pointed out that...well, it had made quite a mess, a hundred feet of paper strung out all over his house.

In other words, somebody would have to clean it up, probably Slim, so maybe I should grit my teeth and accept some responsibility for adding another mess to his life.

So listen up. Right here in front of everyone, I admit that *a mistake had been made*. Shame on the mistake for making itself! And shame on the paper for rolling itself through the house!

Whew, that was tough, but there's more.

Remember the lamp? It was a priceless family heirloom, and it had shattered into a thousand pieces. Ruined. Slim had crashed into it all by himself but had tripped over me, hence I would get blamed.

I needed to come up with a clarification. I began pacing around the porch, rehearsing my story. "Slim, let me begin by saying that I feel terrible about this. It was a beautiful lamp, I mean, the only object in the entire house that wasn't Bachelor Ugly."

Wait. That sounds harsh, but that's usually the way it goes with first drafts, right? You make a first pass, wad it up, throw it away and start another draft.

Second Draft. "Slim, I never had the pleasure of knowing Aunt Olive, but she must have been a wonderful lady, and what a wonderful day it must have been when she gave you that wonderful lamp. Words can hardly express my sadness that you're such a clumsy ox, you tripped over your dog and trashed a family heirloom."

Wait. That one started right but veered off in the wrong direction with "clumsy ox." I continued pacing, composing Draft Three in a fog of deep concentration. This situation was going to require a lot more than "There, there."

I plunged into it.

Third Draft. "Slim, at this very moment, my heart is a mirror image of Aunt Olive's priceless heirloom lamp—a shattered ruin on the Floor of Life. And I understand that you're going to pin the blame on me, just because I happened to be inside the house and you tripped over me.

"I want you to know that it's okay for you to dump all the blame on your dog. Dogs have been putting up with this for centuries. It's what we do for a living. So, bottom line, if you want to be a scrounge, go ahead and tell everyone that it was all my fault. I'm strong enough to handle it."

What do you think? Would it sell? To make it work, I would have to come up with some good visuals: Tragic Ears, Lifeless Tail, Pleading Eyes, and the other body language that would give some emotional pop to the so-forth.

I had a feeling that I could pull it off. Yes, I could sell this!

But at that very moment, I heard odd sounds in the distance, perhaps tires crunching on gravel. My ears shot up and I switched on Scanners. Yes, it was the crunching of gravel, which meant that an unidentified vehicle was approaching the house.

I reached for the microphone of my mind.

"Hank to Drover, over. Tune in, son, we've got a UV coming this way!"

His dreamy eyes drifted down from outer space. "Oh, hi. Did you just get here?"

I lumbered over to him. "I've been here since dirt was invented."

"I'll be derned. What was here before dirt?"

"Drover, don't start this. We've got a UV coming our way."

"A U-who?"

"A UV, not a yoo-hoo, an unidentified vehicle. We're back on Traffic and it's time to launch all dogs. Let's move out!"

I sprang off the porch with a mighty leap, hit engines one and two, and went roaring around the north side of the house. Drover followed, running as fast as his legs would carry him (they were so short, they barely touched the ground) and firing off an occasion squeak. His squeaks fell way short of the heavy ordinance I was pumping out, but it was the best he could do.

The impointant pork is that we launched all available aircraft, went ripping around the north side of the house, and put ourselves in position to intercept the intruder.

Who would it be this time? We had no idea. The mailman? Not likely. He left Slim's mail in the mailbox on the county road and never came to the house. Slim didn't get much mail anyway, just a few bills, a couple of livestock magazines, and the monthly picture show calendar (that was a waste, he never went to the movies), so it probably wasn't the mailman.

Who or whom did that leave?

A pickup cream caking toward the house...a pickup came creeping toward the house, that is, and the "creeping" gave me an uneasy feeling. Friendlies and good guys don't creep around. They drive. The bad guys and the Charlies *creep*.

I dived behind a cedar bush and took cover. We needed to check this out before we got ourselves involved in something heavy. Drover didn't notice that I had gone into hiding and went skipping past, firing off squeaks.

"Psst, over here!"

He stopped and glanced around. "Hello? I thought I heard a snake."

"It's me, over here."

It took him a while, but he finally located me. "Oh, hi. Did you see that snake? He sounded like a big one."

"Get over here and take cover!"

He crept over to the bush, glancing around with big eyes. "Where's the snake?"

53

"Drover, there's no snake. I said 'Psst' to get your attention."

"Oh good, I'm scared of snakes. What are we doing?"

"We're setting up a scout position. We don't dare commit troops until we get some identification on that trespasser."

"Oh, you mean Loper?"

"What?"

"It's Loper."

"What makes you think so?"

"Because Loper's driving."

I took a closer...hm, sure enough, the driver appeared to be the owner of our ranch, and he appeared to be driving one of the ranch pickups. "Nice work, son, you passed."

"It was a test?"

"Exactly. Once a month we go through this little drill to make sure our systems are working."

"How'd I do?"

"Actually, you did pretty well."

"What do you mean, 'actually'?"

"It means you did pretty well and everyone on the staff is shocked."

"Gosh, thanks. So you're proud of me?"

"Oh yes, very proud. Put a few more of those high scores together and we just might find a little promotion for you."

He almost melted. "A promotion, no fooling? Oh goodie!"

"Congratulations, we'll celebrate later. Right now, we have to give Loper an escort to the house."

It was kind of an emotional moment, wasn't it? You bet. As I say, rust is the enemy in this business. It's *very important* that we do those monthly drills to check out our equipment, and Drover had exceeded everyone's expectorations. Very touching.

Anyway, we left the cedar bush, sprinted out in front of the pickup, and gave the boss an escort all the way to the house. We knew that he didn't need help finding his way, but Escort is part of our Regular Service Package and we're glad to do it.

He parked in front of the house and walked up to the porch. I fell in step beside him and gave him a big Good Morning Smile. He seemed preoccupied and didn't notice.

Oh well. Sometimes they speak to the dogs in the morning and sometimes they don't.

He banged on the door. Seconds passed. "Hey, get out of bed!" More seconds passed. He speared me with his eyes and said, "Is he still asleep?"

Huh? Not asleep, but not exactly ready to meet the public either.

"Slowest human I ever met." He banged again.

At last the door swung open, revealing Slim pretty muchly as he had looked the last time I'd seen him, in his long johns and wearing a pack rat's nest on his head.

Oh, and he was holding a jumble of white paper in one hand. Loper scowled. "What's that?"

"Nothing. Can you come back later?"

"No. We need to talk."

Slim tried to close the door but Loper pushed his way into the house. I had been expecting something like this and was ready to make my move. Whilst the door was open a crack, I slithered past Lipper's logs and squirted over to my spot in front of the wood stove.

I slithered past Loper's legs, it should be. In a flash, I was lying on the floor, broadcasting a look that said, "I've been here for hours."

Nobody seemed to notice. Hee hee. Good.

Loper's gaze darted around the house. It looked, well, pretty bad: streams of white bunting, the avalanche from the closet, an overturned table, and the remains of Aunt Olive's lamp. He gave his head a shake. "What happened in here?"

Slim's back stiffened and I think his lip curled. Yes, it did, I saw it, and he growled, "You just had to show up, didn't you? I know you love to catch me at the worst possible times."

"I don't plan it that way. There's just so many opportunities. What happened?"

"I can't explain it."

Loper's eyes roamed. "The lamp?"

"It broke."

"Yes, I believe it did. Ugly color, yellow. Reminds me of a headache."

"Someone gave it to my aunt and she fobbed it off on me. I never got around to hauling it to the dump."

"Well, I think you can now. Is that toilet paper?"

"Yes, it is." Slim's head swung around and his eyes came at me like laser beans. "That's *his* work, and how did he get back inside my house?"

I tried to shrink myself into an inconspicuous pile of hair.

"Hank did all that?"

"Ten four. The dog has talents we never dreamed of."

Loper snorted a laugh. "Well, y'all have been having a lot of fun this morning. Is there any chance you might be able to squeeze in some ranch work? I don't want to interfere, but if there's an opening in your schedule..."

Slim gave his head a shake. "Loper, when you grow up, you might be a comedian, but you ain't there yet. Get to the point."

Loper's grin faded. "Have you heard the weather report?"

"No. I make my own bad news. I don't need any help from the radio."

"Well, you ought to tune into the world once in a while. There's a winter storm moving this way. They're talking about ice and freezing rain."

"When's it due?"

"This afternoon and tonight. We need to get prepared." Loper smirked. "But only if it's handy. If you and Hank need to roll out some more paper or wreck some more lamps, we can put it off till spring."

Slim rolled his eyes. "I don't know how Sally May stands your company. I'll meet you at headquarters as quick as I can get there, and throw that dog out when you leave. Bye."

Slim tromped off to the bedroom and Loper turned a snarly look at me. "I think you've been invited to leave."

Huh? Me? But I just...

"OUT!"

CHAPTER SEVEN

A Crisis in Town

Gee, what a grouch. I'm not the kind of dog who complains about the manners of his people, but sometimes they come across as downright rude, especially in the morning. If a dog has even the slightest snivelinskity, he's likely to get his feelings hurt.

Wait. The word we're looking for is "sensitivity." Now we're truckin'. If a dog has any kind of sensitivity in his nature, it's likely to get stepped on by the rude people on this ranch, such as Slim and Loper.

Anyway, for the second time in the space of thirty minutes, I had been kicked out of the house, and did you hear the way Loper phrased it? "OUT!" He had all the charm of a buzzard. I mean, that's the way you'd expect him to talk to a stray dog or a badger, but you'd suppose...never mind.

Fine. If they didn't want me in the house, I sure didn't need to waste another minute of my life in there. I'm a very busy dog and had better things to do.

By the way, did you happen to notice what Slim said about the destruction of his "precious heirloom" lamp? He didn't even care! He said it was UGLY and he was glad to get rid of it!

Why do I bother worrying about those guys?

Anyway, Loper went back to headquarters, and I found myself back on the porch with Drover. We sat there like stumps for what seemed a year, until Slim finally made his entry into the world. He was wearing clothes this time and carrying something in a grocery sack.

When he saw me, he held up the sack and gave it a shake. Something inside rattled. "I couldn't have wrecked it without your help, pooch."

Okay, the lamp.

We loaded into the pickup and drove the two miles west to headquarters. Since we were running late, Slim drove faster than usual. At one point, going downhill, we got up to twenty miles an hour.

He didn't say a word until we reached the

turnoff to headquarters. There, his gaze began sliding in my direction and I had a feeling that he had something on his mind. Sure enough, he did.

"Thanks to you and your shenanigans, I didn't get my morning coffee. When I don't get my coffee, I ain't my usual charming, lovable self, so try not to do anything ignorant for the rest of the day. Can we make a deal on that?"

Oh brother.

"Raise your right front paw and promise on the memory of your doggie grandma that you won't do anything ignorant until tomorrow morning."

This was so silly! I would NOT raise my right front paw and be part of this nonsense.

"And thanks again for fixing up my place. Now the boss knows for sure that I live in a monkey house."

He just goes on and on.

"Who knows, with all your good help, maybe he'll cut my wages in half."

What can you say? I turned my back on him and looked out the window and ignored him for the rest of the trip. Lucky for me, we didn't have far to go.

But he did get one thing right. When he doesn't get his morning coffee, he isn't fit to live with. The sooner I could get away from him, the better I would like it.

When we pulled up behind the house, I hopped out of the pickup and noticed a chill in the air. The wind had shifted to the north and angry gray clouds were moving across the sun. Slim noticed it too, and turned up the collar on his coat. "Well, here it comes. Red sky at morning, sailor take warning."

Loper came out the back door, tying a knot in his blue wild rag. At the yard gate, he said, "Glad you could make it."

"I got here as fast as I could."

"Some day we ought to work up a race between you and a glacier." Loper pulled a piece of paper out of his pocket. "We've got a long list of things to do: feed hay to all the pastures, chop ice on the stock tanks, test the generator, bring in firewood..."

Sally May opened the back door. "Loper, phone call for you."

"Hon, take a number. We've got two days' work lined up before this storm."

"It's Deputy Kile. I think you'd better take it."

Loper shook his head and grumbled, "Great." He hurried back into the house. When he returned a few minutes later, his face was long, dark, and solemn. I noticed that right away. I mean, some dogs study faces and some don't, Drover for example.

Slim noticed too. "Well, did Deputy Kile bring glad tidings of great joy?"

"No, and our plans just got changed."

"Bad news or awful?"

"Bad enough. Some of our wheat pasture steers strayed. The electric fence must have shorted out."

Slim nodded. "It's the tumbleweeds. They pile up on the wire when the wind blows, then they get wet and short out the current. I told you this was going to happen."

"When did you tell me that?"

"The last time we rode through those steers. Don't you remember? The wind was blowing hard and the tumbleweeds were rolling. You thought it was a bunch of feral hogs running across the field."

"I did not."

"Well, one of us did, and I said that one of these days, those tumbleweeds were going to short out the fence."

"What's your point?"

Slim hitched up his jeans. "Let the record show that I saw this one coming. How many steers got out?"

"Ten head."

"Where'd they end up?"

"You'll like this. They're on the Twitchell golf course."

Slim's eyes popped open. "The golf course! Good honk, what if they go into town and start eating peoples' yards, or walk down Main Street?"

"Deputy Kile was concerned about that. He mentioned damages, fines, law suits, and jail time."

Slim shook his head and whistled under his breath. "And we've got a storm moving in. Well, we'd better saddle horses and head north."

There was a long moment of silence, as Loper rocked up and down on his toes and studied the sky. "You know, you're always belly-aching about how you never get to do cowboy work. This sounds like a cowboy job."

"It sounds like a wreck waiting for some fool to show up."

Loper laid a hand on Slim's shoulder. "I've had to make an executive decision here. Someone needs to stay at the ranch, hay the cattle and chop ice, and take care of the lowly stuff. I've decided to let you take the glory job."

Slim jerked away from Loper's hand. "If I'd had any idea that you were listening, I would have kept my mouth shut about the cowboy stuff."

Loper grinned. "Yes, but you didn't, and here

we are."

"Loper, you're...I don't even have words. 'Skunk' is way too nice. What in the cat hair am I supposed to do with ten head of steers running a-loose on the Twitchell municipal golf course?"

"Luckily, we've got a gen-u-wine old-school cowpuncher to figure that out. If it was me, I'd take the big gooseneck trailer. Maybe you can load 'em and haul 'em back to wheat pasture and fix the fence. Deputy Kile said he'd meet you at the golf course, and he's bringing some portable corral panels." He checked his watch. "You'd better saddle a horse, you're burning daylight."

"Loper..."

"Be happy in your work, and let me know how it goes." A veil of sadness fell over his face. "Boy, I wish I was a cowboy."

He walked away, got into his pickup, and drove to the stack lot to load up bales of alfalfa. Slim stood speechless. "I ain't believing this. Me and my big mouth."

What followed was something for the record books. Slim Chance lit a fire under his tail and began moving at a pace we had seldom seen, I mean, the man was actually rushing around! He hooked up the 24-foot gooseneck trailer and roared down to the corrals.

Drover and I went down to the saddle shed and watched the show. Wow, it was something to see. This was a new Slim Chance! He threw a saddle on Snips, who was still half asleep and chewing his morning hay, then he trotted back into the saddle shed and grabbed two extra catch ropes.

Drover and I sat outside the fence, watching. Drover said, "What's wrong with him?"

"Well, he has to do some work today."

"Work. What a bummer."

"Exactly my thought. If he'd been halfway civilized this morning, I might have volunteered to help, but I'll be very happy to wave goodbye and watch him leave."

"Yeah, me too. It makes me glad I'm just a mutt, not a cowdog. Hee hee. It's too cold for work."

"Exactly right. We'll take the day off and try to stay warm. If Alfred comes outside, we'll play with him for a while, then take a nice long nap."

"Oh goodie. Boy, I love naps."

Slim opened the saddle lot gate and led his horse to the trailer. I happened to be sitting near the back of the trailer, minding my own business, when I heard him growl, "Move!"

No manners, no soft tone, no "please." Fine, I could move. He threw open the trailer gate and

loaded his poor, sleepy horse, who had no idea what kind of crazy things he was being sent out to do.

Slim slammed the gate and secured the latch. He saw me sitting there. "You ain't invited."

Oh really? Well, that was just fine with me. For his information, I had already planned out my day and IT DIDN'T INCLUDE HIM.

CHAPTER EIGHT

I Get Shanghaied

Okay, where were we? Oh yes, a cold windy day that was fixing to get colder and windier. The boss was sending Slim Chance to town on some bit of cowboy foolishness...what was it? Something about tumbleweeds on the golf course. Slim was supposed to gather up tumbleweeds and, I don't know, feed them to a bunch of hogs that were playing golf.

It sounded like a screwball assignment and I had no interest in being a part of it. Slim begged me to go along, but I turned him down flat. He had behaved in such a rude and crabby manner, I had no intention of spending another minute in his company.

He didn't deserve the warmth and companionship of a loyal dog. You know what he deserved? A thirty-five pound snapping turtle! Snapping turtles have a thick shell, ugly green eyes, and no personality, which makes them a perfect match for Slim Chance when he doesn't get his morning cup of coffee.

No sir, I had my own schedule and my own list of things to do when we got Slim off the ranch. I would check the yard gate for breakfast scraps, run Sally May's rotten little cat up the nearest tree, volunteer a few minutes of quality time with Little Alfred, and spend the rest of the day in a warm spot, listening to the moan of the north wind.

So there we were down at the saddle shed, Drover and I. Slim had just loaded his horse into the stock trailer and was about leave us in peace. He trotted off to the pickup and I went to work on an itchy spot on my left ear. I had given it three good hacks with my left hind leg, when I realized...huh?

Slim was back, standing over me, and giving me a peculiar look. And he said—this is a direct quote—he said, "On second thought, I might need your help on this deal."

My help? Sorry, I had already made plans, and he could forget...

"Come on, pooch, nice doggie."

Alarm bells went off and I began edging away.

I mean, this wasn't rocket surgery. When they start that "nice doggie" business, it always means trouble for the dogs. He made a dive for me and, naturally, I ran.

"Hank, come back here!"

Forget that, Charlie.

I ran and he chased. We made a lap around the pickup and trailer, and he kept coming, so I squirted myself under the pickup—as any normal, healthy American dog would have done.

I thought that might be the end of it, but then I saw his awful grinning face full of sharp teeth. "Hi, puppy, how'd you like to go to town with old Slim? We'll have some fun."

We would NOT have some fun, because I had no intention of...

What a cheap trick! He reached out and grabbed a hind leg before I could take countermeasures. He dragged me out of my safe haven and pitched me into the cab of the pickup.

And Drover? He vanished, I mean like a puff of smoke in the wind. I don't know how he does that, the little weasel, but the bottom line was that I had been shanghaied and pressed into service.

And off we went on some crazy mission. I went straight to the shotgun side of the pickup seat, as far away from Slim as I could get, and turned my back on him. He had kidnapped me against my will, so I would give him a good and proper SHUNNING. Yes sir, he would get none of my usual...

"You want some beef jerky?"

...warmth and charm. Beef jerky? Absolutely not! Did he think I could be bribed and bought off with...sniff sniff...actually, it smelled pretty good. I mean, a guy forgets how good beef jerky smells in the morning.

He made his own jerky, you know, and soaked the strips of beef in a concoction made of liquid smoke, roostershire sauce, and exotic spices. In a pickup cab that usually smelled of gasoline and

dirty socks, it released a powerful...

Okay, I would resume diplomatic relations just enough to end the Shunning Procedure. I turned away from the window and slurped at him...looked at him, that is, and licked my chops.

He held something in his right hand. It was brownish-red and resembled a dried mouse carcass, but that was just the normal appearance of his jerky. It never looked as good as it slurped... as good as it tasted.

I, uh, scooted closer to him and found my thoughts drifting back to happier times. He really wasn't such a bad guy. I mean, morning had never been his best time of day, and let's be fair, sometimes I did things that brought out the crabby side of his Inner Bean, such as...well, waking him up with a fire alarm when the house wasn't actually on fire.

And that business with the toilet paper? Bad idea, poor judgment, and I was feeling pretty bad about it.

I edged closer. He held the jerky under my slurp...under my nose and moved it up and down. As if by magic, my nose followed —up and down, around and around.

He chuckled. He was enjoying this and in a weird sort of way, so was I, but didn't we need to reach some kind of resolution? And wasn't he supposed to be driving? When you're moving down a country road in a pickup and pulling a gooseneck trailer, somebody ought to be...

Good grief, we were heading toward the ditch! I barked. He turned his eyes back to the road and jerked the wheel just in time to miss the only tree within two miles.

I struck like a bolt of lightning and bagged the jerky.

Hee hee!

He gave me a sour look. "Hey, we were supposed to share that."

Yeah, well, tough toenails. Don't give your dog more temptation than he can handle.

Great stuff! Slim wasn't chef enough to boil an egg, but the guy had a talent for making jerky. It was a little chewy, but hey, if you can't handle beef jerky, you're not a Texas dog. Move to California and eat oatmeal.

Fellers, I put it away, chewed it up and rammed it down the pipe. In spite of himself, old Slim seemed pleased. "Well, I guess you liked it."

Oh yes, but the important thing was that the experience had cemented our relationship, taken it to a new and higher level. All the morning's strife and bitterness just melted away. I dived into his lap and gave him three Bonus Licks on the face.

"Quit."

Hey, we were pals again!

We reached the blacktop highway, turned right, and headed towards town at seventy miles an hour. I remained in his lap and helped him drive until we rolled past the city limits sign. There, he invited me to move.

"We're in the Big City now and I'd better pay attention to business." We coasted past Waterhole 83 and his eyes scanned an expanse of brown grass east of the highway. "Well, there they are."

Who? I studied the field of grass up ahead. Oh, maybe this was the golf course and...what were we looking for? Tumbleweeds and hogs? Yes, there they were, I saw them, only...wait, not hogs, ten head of steers. Forget the tumbleweeds.

Maybe you had forgotten some of the details of this assignment. Not me. We had come on a mission to do something with ten head of steers that had strayed from a wheat field east of town.

"And there's Bobby."

Who? He seemed to be looking toward a white pickup that was pulling a green 16-foot bumper-hitch stock trailer. (It's kind of amazing that a dog would notice all this stuff, isn't it?) We left the highway, crossed the ditch, and drove out on the golf course, toward the pickup.

A man wearing a uniform and a felt hat got out. Okay, Chief Deputy Kile. Had you forgotten? Not me. He was the one who had started all of this with a phone call. You need to pay attention.

Slim shut off the motor and we got out. Slim looked up at the cloudy sky. "Freezing mist. That ain't good." We walked over to the deputy who was writing in some kind of book. Slim said, "Morning."

The deputy didn't look up. "Morning."

"What are you doing?"

"Taking notes."

"On what?"

"This case. I talked to Judge McKinley this morning. He thinks he can work out a plea deal with the county attorney and get you off with ten years in prison. That's with good behavior. If you mouth off, like you normally do, it'll be thirty years of busting rock for Uncle Bud."

Slim gave his head a sad shake. "Bobby, most of the law enforcement officers in this county work day and night to build a good reputation. Then you show up and it all goes to blazes. You ain't funny, so don't even try."

Deputy Kile cackled and put away his writing pad. "Glad you could come. Beautiful day. What are you going to do with these steers?"

That was the Big Question that hung over us, and you don't know the answer. I know the answer but I'm not going to tell you, so you'd better keep reading.

CHAPTER NINE

This Is Very Bad

Okay, there we were, standing out in the freezing drizzle on the Twitchell marsupial golf course. The *municipal* golf course, let us say. Mun-i-ci-pal. It's a four-cylinder word that means... I don't know what it means, but that's what they called it, the *municipal golf course.*

And we faced a heavy decision: what were we going to do with ten head of stray cattle that weren't supposed to be running loose on the edge of town?

Slim pulled on his chin. "Did you bring portable panels?"

"Yes sir, ten of 'em. My wife had to help me load 'em in the trailer and she's permanently mad at you."

"Bobby…"

"She's going to send you a bill for five hundred dollars."

Slim ignored him. "Well, let's set 'em up. I brought a horse. I'll pen 'em, we'll load 'em in my trailer, and be on our way." He gazed at the sky. "Before this place turns into an ice skating rink."

They opened the gate on the deputy's trailer and started lugging the portable panels. I was there to supervise. "Okay, boys, hook those panels together and make a catch pen. Good. Bring another one and try to hurry, I'm freezing out here."

"Hank, get out of the way!"

"Sure glad you brought the dog."

"Bobby, hush."

I had to keep a close eye on those guys, I mean, it's hard to find good help these days.

They hooked the panels together, and when we were done, we had a nice little catch pen that would hold ten head. We left the pen open on the north end and made a wing with the pickups and trailers.

Slim unloaded his horse and began tightening the cinches. Next thing I knew, the horse and I were glaring at each other. He was a big red dun named Snips, and I had never cared for him. He was your typical ranch horse, only moreso. He had an attitude, don't you see, thought he was hot stuff, and he had tried to bite my tail off on several occasions.

Have I mentioned that I don't like horses? I don't like horses, have no use for 'em at all, and Snips and I glared daggers at each other.

He didn't look so happy, standing out there in the freezing drizzle. He was shivering and had a hump in his back that made him look like a camel. Naturally, I was concerned.

"Hey Snips, how's it going, pal? Nice day for a ride, huh?" He pinned down his ears and made a lunge at me. "Ha, ha! A little slow there, Trigger. I guess you've been spending too much time with your nose in the hay feeder." He made another snap and missed. "Nope, half a step behind. Loose fifty pounds and we'll try it again."

Hee hee. Boy, I love heckling horses! I mean, they think they're so superior to the rest of us.

Slim stuffed his boot into the left stirrup, took a double grip on the horn, and lugged himself into the saddle. He was so bundled up with clothes, he didn't look very graceful. Oh, and he drilled me with a hard gaze.

"Hank, don't mess with my horse. If you get me bucked off, we're going to have words." He turned to Deputy Kile. "Keep a handle on Bozo. He might help us later on, but I don't need him chasing the stock."

"Can you ride without falling off?"

Slim chuckled. "We never know. Ask me in fifteen minutes."

Slim stuck Fat Boy with the spurs and they trotted north, toward the cattle. Snips wrung his tail, pinned back his ears, and humped up in a halfway buck. What did I tell you? They're all that way, arrogant and lazy. I'm not kidding. They think their whole purpose in life is to loaf around the hay feeder and EAT. Make 'em do an honest day's work and...never mind. Don't get me started on horses.

Deputy Kile and I got into his pickup. He turned up the heater and we watched the show, and by the way, that wasn't so easy, because the freezing drizzle was making ice on the windshield. Deputy Kile turned on the defroster and windshield wipers. That helped.

Slim approached the steers. They raised their heads and watched. He slowed his crowbait...his horse, that is, to a walk and started pushing the cattle toward the portable pen.

Uh oh. One of them, a red bald-faced calf, was high-headed and you could see what was on his mind. He wanted to make a break. This close to town, that wouldn't be funny. Slim moved Snips into the right position and kept the herd moving toward the pen.

Deputy Kile nodded. "Good move." He looked at me and seemed surprised that I was, well, sitting in his lap. Why not? I mean, his lap had been totally empty, even desolate, almost begging for a dog to fill it with warmth and friendship. And the pickup seat was cold.

I went to Slow Taps on the tail section and his voice broke the silence. "Hank..."

Yes sir?

"Where did you get your smell?"

My smell?

"I'm not a fussy man, but you really stink." He pushed me away.

You know, it's sad when little things break up a friendship. Hey, I had ridden most of the way into town in Slim's lap and he hadn't said a word about my so-called "smell."

Oh well, back to the main event. Slim eased the steers into the catch pen, stepped off his horse, and dragged the panels together, closing up the pen. Deputy Kile said, "He got 'em."

Well, this was turning out better than anyone could have expected. I mean, it could have been a real mess if the cattle had spooked and gone on a wild romp through town—while freezing drizzle was putting a coat of ice on everything.

And by the way, it WAS. We needed to finish the job and get out of there.

Slim backed the stock trailer up to the catch pen, then he and Deputy Kile unhooked two panels to make a gate, and baling-wired the panels to the trailer.

Are you following all of this? If not, don't worry. It was a simple procedure but hard to explain, and I was there to make sure they didn't mess anything up. The important thing is that with my help, they rigged up the pen so that we could load the steers into the stock trailer.

At that very moment, Deputy Kile heard someone calling him on the sheriff's department radio. He trotted to the pickup and spoke into the microphone. He returned wearing a frown. "Slim, they've got a cattle truck jack-knifed on the highway north of town. I've got to go. Can you handle it from here?"

Slim smirked. "Bobby, when you leave, it's like two good men showed up to help. Thanks for the panels. Hank and I can finish up."

The deputy unhooked his trailer and left in a hurry, his red light flashing and his siren screeching. Wow. It was impressive, and you know what? It kind of reminded me of my own work back at the ranch, roaring up to the county road to intercept the mailman and sending him on his way.

Anyway, law enforcement went speeding off, and Slim and I were left to finish the job. He climbed over the panels and got into the pen with the steers. "Okay, pooch, it's time for you to make a hand. Let's load 'em up."

Aye, aye, sir!

I slithered my bad self under the bottom rail, went into Stealthy Crouch, and beamed a cold cowdog glare at the steers. "Okay, you morons, face the trailer and load up. Slackers have to deal with me. Move it!"

Sometimes they cooperate and sometimes I have to do some persuading with the Nip Heels Procedure. This time, by George, everything was copacetic and all systems worked. The little dummies hopped into the trailer and that was that.

Slim reached for the trailer gate, swung it shut, and was trying to secure the latch, when... uh oh. Remember that high-headed red steer? He hopped into the trailer, ran to the front, did a one-eighty, and came back at a high rate of speed.

He center-punched the gate at twenty miles an hour. He might have been a "little dummy," but he was a pretty big little dummy, about six hundred pounds of muscle and meanness, and when he crashed into the gate, bad things happened.

The gate flew open, knocking Slim into me and sending both of us rolling across the frozen golf course grass. It knocked us both about half-silly, but I managed to croak, "You'd better shut the trailer gate or they'll all jump out!"

Slim struggled to his feet and managed to slam the gate shut and secure the latch. At that point, we both turned our attention to the...yipes, this steer was an outlaw in a bad mood. We're talking glowing red eyes, smoke coming out of his nostrils, quivering with malice, and pawing up frozen dirt with his hooves.

HERE HE CAME! And fellers, he cleared the ring, in spite of my best efforts to stun him with some Dog Karate. I mean, he was big enough and mean enough to eat Dog Karate for breakfast, and he tried.

It was a sad spectacle and a dark time for our ranch. Slim climbed over the icy fence and I scrambled under it, and we watched while the demented steer slammed into the trailer gate and

hit the portable pen in three places, then...

This was bad, so prepare yourself. The nutcase steer wasn't able to destroy the equipment, so he circled the pen and leaped into the air, straddled a panel (and bent it), and tumbled to the ground— outside the pen. There, he got back on his feet, made a razzoo at Snips, and raced off to the north...TOWARD DOWNTOWN TWITCHELL!

Oh no! That had been our worst nightmare from the very start of this mission, that we'd have livestock running through town.

And it was happening, before our very eyes.

CHAPTER TEN

Good Nutrition Is Very Important

A re you still with me? If you decide to quit and go to bed, I can't blame you. I mean, cowboys and their dogs wake up in the middle of the night, having bad dreams about this sort of thing.

And don't forget about the ice storm. It was getting worse by the second.

I shot a glance at Slim. His chin had fallen down on his chest and his eyes had turned into empty holes. And as if all of this weren't bad enough, his horse started mouthing off.

"Oh, nice work, doggie, nice work!"

I whirled around and saw him grinning, and we're talking about one of those big ugly horse grins with green alfalfa-stained teeth showing beneath fat lips. Nobody does horse grins better than a horse.

I tried to melt him with a glare and wanted to deliver a slashing reply, but, well, found myself without anything slashing to say. All I could think of was, "Oh yeah?"

"That's why we tie up the dogs and leave 'em at the house. Now I have to clean up your mess, as usual."

I thundered toward him...two steps. "Oh yeah? Well, you're a fat, arrogant fraud of a horse with green-stained teeth!"

"Woo, poison! Come two steps closer, puppy, and I'll show you what green-stained teeth can do to a dog's tail."

I was trembling with righteous anger, aching to give the jerk the thrashing he so richly deserved, but...well, this was a business situation and one of us had to show some maturity. I made a wide loop around him (don't forget, they can kick a dog into next week) and joined my poor, discouraged comrade, who was leaning against the pen and staring off to the north.

I jumped up on his thigh and beamed him Looks of Deepest Sympathy. He rubbed me on the head and tried to smile. "Well, we got whipped on that one, pooch. Now it's time to cowboy-up. I have no idea how this is going to turn out, but you stay here with the pickup."

Yes sir.

He walked over to the smart-aleck horse, tightened the front cinch, and climbed into the saddle. He untied his catch rope and built a loop. "Don't follow me, Hank. Do you copy?"

Roger that, got it.

"I don't need a dog to make this deal even worse than it is."

Right, I understood. No hard feelings.

"Hop in the back of the pickup and try to look intelligent."

Yes sir.

He turned his pampered, mouthy horse and trotted off toward town. I gave him three minutes' head start, then did what any normal, red-blooded, patriotic American cowdog would have done.

I FOLLOWED HIM, of course!

Did he actually think I was going to sit in the pickup? Forget that. Not only did he need a friend, but I had a score to settle with his horse. I wasn't about to let a horse get the credit for cleaning up a mess I didn't make.

Does that make sense? Maybe not, but sometimes Life doesn't make sense and we just have to carry on. The point is, I wasn't going to sit in the pickup while my cowboy pal was off on a dangerous mission, and that was final.

Okay, let's get on with this before we get too scared to move. The golf course lay on the southeastern edge of town and the steer was heading north. So was Slim because...well, because he was following the steer, of course, and maybe that's obvious.

The point is, after the steer had run half a mile across the golf course, he ran out of golf course. The empty grass pasture came to an end and became the south end of town, with houses and yards, streets, cars, kids, and all the other things you find in a town. In other words, yipes.

The steer left the golf course and trotted out on Main Street, but this wasn't the same Main Street it had been only an hour before. Do you know why? Because all that freezing drizzle had formed a layer of ice on the pavement, and the dumbbell steer didn't figure it out until he was out on the middle of the street.

I held my breath and watched. He was trotting right down the middle of the street, I mean following the yellow stripes, and a car was approaching from the north. The driver hit the brakes and went into a skid. The steer stopped in the middle of the street, stared at the oncoming car, said, "Duh," and tried to scramble out of the way.

He got the "scramble" part right, I mean, he looked like scrambled eggs out there on the ice, four legs churning and going nowhere. He went tail-over-tea kettle down on the pavement and... hang on, this is getting scary...the car slid toward him and...

Do you really want to go on with this? You know how I am: give the children a thrill now and then, but go easy on the heavy-duty scary parts. Actually, I think we'll be okay on this one, because I was there and saw the whole thing, and I can report that the car missed him by about two inches.

Slim had stopped his horse on the east side of Main Street and watched the whole thing, probably holding his breath and wondering "what in the cat hair" he was going to do next. That's just the way he would have said it, by the way, "what in the cat hair." I can't tell you what "cat hair" had to do with it, and my own preference would have been to leave cats out of it, but that was the way he talked.

I had been following along at a distance, more than slightly aware that I had ignored Slim's order to stay in the back of the pickup, and that he might not be thrilled when I showed up. But this deal had gotten out of hand and somebody had to step up and take charge, right?

Hencely, while Slim was watching the events on Main Street, I kicked up the jets and raced toward him. When I arrived at his side, I went to Full Air Brakes and, oops, ha ha, you'd probably forgotten about the icy conditions, right? Me too, lost all four feet, and slid right under Slim's horse, I mean surrounded on all sides by feet and hooves that could kick the snot out of a dog.

See, your average horse doesn't enjoy having a dog in that position, under his belly and amongst his legs.

For a moment I didn't dare breathe. Snips' nose appeared in my field of vision, then his eyes, I mean, he was looking back at me through his front legs, which was a little weird because his head was upside-down.

Gulp. Somehow, I had to talk my way out of this mess.

"Hey, Snips, how's it going, buddy? Listen, we've got an awkward situation here, and let me begin by saying that it happened by accident. I understand that you don't enjoy having dogs between your legs, and I want to assure you that

I'm not thrilled to be here, so if you'll just hang loose for a second, I'll relocate my location. How does that sound?"

He didn't move or kick, and I crept out of the Danger Zone. Whew, that was a close one! Right away, I saw his big green-tooth grin and he said, "You're such a loser."

"Oh yeah? If I'm such a loser..."

"Hank!"

Huh? Oops, that was Slim. Yes, there he was, sitting in the saddle and, well, glaring at me.

"Hammerhead, I told you to stay at the pickup!"

Pickup? What pickup? Oh, *that* pickup? Well, I must have misunderstood. We got our signals crossed. A breakdown in communications.

"Go to the pickup, scram, scat!"

Obviously, he was trying to tell me something but, gee, it wasn't coming through.

"Noodle brain. Disobedient whelp of a dog." He shook his head and heaved a big sigh. "But I've got bigger problems than you. If I don't get that steer turned around, he's going to be in downtown Twitchell."

Sure enough, the red steer had survived a near-miss in the middle of the street and was now standing right in front of the Dixie Dog Drive-in. A woman walked out the front door, holding a Big Beefy in one hand and drink in the other, and almost had a run-away when she saw the steer. She screamed, dropped the burger, and ran back inside.

Hmm. Big Beefy.

Anyway, the steer slipped and slid, and headed north, toward downtown. Slim nudged Snips with spurs and they stepped out on the icy street, following the steer as fast as they dared. I, uh, found my path bending to the left, on a course that promised to take me...

You ever eat a Big Beefy? Best burger in town, everybody says so. I had never eaten one myself, but I'd been in the pickup several times when Slim was gulping one down, and I can tell you, they smelled GREAT.

I know, we had important business to take care of, but that was the whole point. *Important business demands good nutrition.* If a dog's going to set out on a dangerous mission, he needs to be performing at his very best, right? You bet.

So for the sake of the mission, I altered course and headed straight for the nutrition. I could see it now, wrapped in thin white paper and lying unattended on the sidewalk. Ten feet away, I

began picking it up on Snifforadar. Oh my!

Just as I got there, the door opened and I found myself looking into the eyes of the lady. Her lip curled into a snarl and she said, "That's my burger, don't you dare!"

Dare what? She didn't make herself clear, so I...well, snatched up the nutrition and ran like a striped ape.

"Bring that back! I'm going to call the

dogcatcher!"

I couldn't understand exactly what she was trying to say. Maybe she'd noticed the ice and how slick it was, and by George, she was right, it was very slick. I hoped she would watch her step.

Anyway, I was back on the job, trucking north to catch up with Slim and the steer. Eating the burger...that is, absorbing the nutrition while trotting on an icy sidewalk was no easy ball of wax, in fact, it was very difficult. No ordinary dog could have done it. It required just the right combination of biting, chewing, and gulping, and there was no time to sift out the onions, pickles, tomatoes, or lettuce.

Or the tissue paper. This was a hurry-up deal and everything went to the Department of Nutrition.

Borp. Best burger I ever ate.

CHAPTER ELEVEN

Rodeo On Main Street

Now where were we? Oh yes, on a Top Priority mission to do something about a deranged red baldface steer before he caused a wreck in downtown Twitchell, because that's exactly where he was heading.

This same outlaw steer had already caused problems at the Dixie Dog Drive-in. We'd gotten word that because of the steer, an innocent lady had lost her burger, I mean, stolen right there in daily broadlight by some mutt, and she was going to turn him in to the dogcatcher.

Actually, that was something to worry about, because...well, for various reasons we didn't need the dogcatcher snooping around in our business.

By the time I caught up with Slim and his

crow-bait horse, they were in the very center of the Twitchell shopping district, two solid blocks of shops and stores, including the drug store, the picture show, Foxie's Lady's Wear, Leonard's Saddle Shop, and all the rest. Huge metropolitan area.

I noticed that Snips was moving in a cautious manner on the ice, with short steps. "Hey, Snippers, has anyone ever told you that you walk like Tinker Bell?"

"Shaddap."

"You'd look cute in a tutu."

He made a snap at me, but I saw it coming and ducked. "Still half a step slow, pal. Keep on your diet and we'll try again sometime. Hee hee!"

Mad? Oh, he was fuming, and I loved every second of it. Any time I can irritate a horse, it makes my day.

But back to the business. Things were not looking good. The steer had been running down the middle of Main Street, but something spooked him and he cut left and headed straight for Foxie's Lady's Wear. Good grief, if someone opened the door, he might actually run inside! I mean, he was standing right in front of the store, looking in the display window.

By this time, people were coming out of stores,

watching, staring, pointing, and talking. Slim was shaking his head and muttering. He didn't know what to do. Nobody did.

Just then, a lady walked out of the drug store, across the street from Foxie's. She wore jeans, red roper boots, and a fleece-lined coat, and she was kind of cute, I mean, a dog notices things like that. I looked closer and there was something familiar about her.

Holy smokes, it was Miss Viola! Remember her? Cutest, sweetest gal in all of Ochiltree County, in fact, in all of Texas, and get this: she was CRAZY about me! No kidding. Okay, she liked Slim too, and wore his engagement ring with the microscopic diamond, but out of all the dogs in the world, I was her very most favorite.

I barked. She looked up. "Hank?"

See? What did I tell you? She adored me, and I raced toward her and, well, almost knocked her down on the ice. "What are you doing here?"

I turned my nose toward Slim and barked, and that's when she saw him, ahorseback in the middle of the Twitchell shopping district. I'm sure she thought that was pretty strange. She looked both ways and started across the icy street.

"Slim, is that you?"

He turned in the saddle. "Viola? Good honk! Man alive, I'm glad to see you! I've got a little favor to ask."

"What on earth...?"

He gave her a quick summary of the day's events. "I'm going to have to stick a loop on that steer."

"You're going to rope him, on this ice? Slim..."

"Got to, before he hurts someone. Listen, my pickup and trailer are parked on the golf course. Drive to it and bring it back. With any luck, I'll have the steer roped and maybe we can load him in the trailer."

"Oh my. Can you do that with all this ice? What if your horse falls?"

"We'll take it one wreck at a time. Be careful driving, and take the dog, would you?"

Wow, did you hear that? I had been assigned to escort Miss Viola, and to protect her from ice and snow, and snowy ice, and all the villains that lurked in big cities like Twitchell. What a deal!

Viola and I crossed the street and loaded up in her daddy's pickup. Uh oh. The pavement had gotten so slick, she couldn't back out of the parking space. The tires spun and whined, but we didn't move.

I barked. "Put it in four-wheel drive."

It's kind of amazing that a dog would know all this stuff, isn't it? You bet, but in the Texas Panhandle, they expect a dog to know just about everything involved in running a...borp.

Excuse me. They expect us to know just about everything involved in running a ranch —cattle, horses, Traffic, Special Crimes, even pickups.

Viola gave me a peculiar look. "Have you been eating *onions*?"

Onions? Oh that. Yes, onions, pickles, and a whole load of good stuff that came with the Big Beefy. Put it in four-wheel drive and let's get going.

She reached down and pulled a lever down one notch, into "4-H," which meant "four-wheel drive, high range." We backed away from the curb and headed south, toward the golf course.

While Viola drove, I looked out the back window at the drama in front of Foxie's. Slim held his loop shoulder-high and eased Snips closer to the steer. The steer shook his head and wrung his tail, then turned to run. The sidewalk was slick and he went down, and that was exactly the shot Slim wanted.

How did I know? Well, a dog knows, that's all I can tell you.

He delivered a perfect loop, soft and open and turned in such a way that the left side of the loop tilted downward. In other words, when it arrived, it was almost vertical...and the steer stepped right into it!

Hey, even without my help, Slim had one-looped him, and I can tell you from experience that he wasn't always a One-Loop Cowboy. Believe me, the dogs know the true stories about roping adventures. Sometimes his loops caught nothing but dirt and fresh air, but this time, fellers, he had dialed the right number.

He jerked his slack, zipped the loop tight around the steer's neck, and dallied the rope around the saddle horn. The deed was done!

Exactly what he would do with a six hundred pound steer on an icy sidewalk in downtown Twitchell, I didn't know, and by that time, he had disappeared from view. He was on his own, without a dog to give him comfort and advice.

I wished him the best. In the meantime, Viola and I were going to run away to...I don't know, to a big castle in the Alps and sit in front of a roaring fireplace, and she was going to rub my ears until we were happily ever-afterly.

Or maybe not. We had things to do.

She drove as fast as she could on the icy street and we finally made it to the golf course and loaded up in Slim's pickup. The seat had been set

for a long-legged man and she couldn't get the seat-changer to work. Her legs were so short, they could hardly reach the pedals, but she mashed on the clutch, put the pickup in first gear and four-wheel drive, and off we went, bouncing across the golf course with nine head of steers in the trailer.

We made it to Main Street and headed north. The bumpy ride across the ditch released a cloud of dust from the heater vents. She fanned the air and coughed. "Bachelors."

When we made it back to the shopping district, we saw Slim and the steer on the sidewalk in front of Foxie's. The steer was at the end of the rope, trying to get traction on the ice, and Snips was hunkered down, trying to hold his ground.

Viola slowed down and studied the situation. We were in the east lane, heading north. Slim and the steer were on the west side of the street. To get the trailer close enough for Slim to load the steer, she would have to park on the wrong side of the street, in the path of southbound traffic.

She chewed her lip for a moment and said, "Well, here goes." She whipped the steering wheel to the left, crossed the center line, and parked in front of Foxie's. Gulp. We were on the wrong side of the street, which was also a major highway, and if a cattle truck came barreling through town...

Pretty scary, huh? You bet, but guess who appeared at that very moment: Chief Deputy Kile! He was coming back from the accident north of town and saw what was happening. He sized it up the situation, turned on his flashing lights, parked his pickup in the southbound lane, and jumped out.

He turned toward Slim and yelled, "I leave you alone for half an hour and look what happens!" Then he started directing traffic into the other lane.

Viola and I dived out of the pickup and hurried over to Slim. He had his rope dallied around the saddle horn and looked pretty solemn.

"Okay, Viola, get inside the trailer and push the calves to the front. Close the middle gate and leave the back gate open. I'll try to drag this steer into the trailer, if my horse can stand up on the ice."

Viola ran to the trailer and got the steers moved to the front and closed the middle gate. Slim turned Snips away from the steer, poked him with spurs, and told him to get up. The steer fought the rope, of course, and Snips was stumbling around on the icy sidewalk, but they made some progress. Slim got the horse lined up on the left side of the trailer and Snips dug in and pulled.

This was a "half-top" stock trailer, which means that the front-half was covered with a roof and the back-half had an open top. You might not see the importance of that, so let me explain. You can drag calves into a half-top trailer, but the technique doesn't work in a fully covered trailer.

As I've said, if you have any questions about ranch work, ask the dog.

Okay, just for a moment, the steer quit struggling and caught his breath. Slim slacked his rope, flipped it over the top rail on the trailer, dallied up again, and told Snips to haul the mail.

They were in the right position to load the calf and by that time Deputy Kile had joined us. He got behind the steer, put his shoulder against his rump, and pushed. Viola joined in and twisted his tail.

The steer's tail, that is, not Deputy Kile's. He didn't have one.

On a normal day, Snips would have made easy work out of this. He was a big stout horse and I had watched him haul many a calf into a trailer. I'll even admit that he was pretty good at it, but the steer was fighting the rope and Snips…I don't know, maybe he was nervous about the ice or maybe he had run out of ambition, but something wasn't working.

Slim yelled, "Hank, bite the calf on the heels!"

My mind tumbled. Everyone was depending on me and I had to do something, but what? Then it came to me—not biting heels but something else, a daring new approach. I had never tried it before, but it just might work.

Keep reading. You won't believe this part.

CHAPTER TWELVE

Incredible Ending, Just Amazing

Okay, there we were in downtown Twitchell and I had to do something to motivate a slacker of a horse. I raced around in front of Snips and gave him a disgusted look.

"Snips, this is pathetic. You're twice the size of that steer. Pull him into the trailer!"

"Shaddap!"

"You know what? Alfred's Welsh pony could do a better job than you."

His lip rose, exposing his big alfalfa-stained teeth. "Take a hike, mutt-fuzz, I don't have time for your big mouth."

"Oh yeah? Well, here's an idea." I turned my backside to him and dusted the end of his nose with the tip of my tail. "Ten bucks says you can't

110

bite my tail."

His eyes grew wide, I mean huge, and he roared, "Oh, you've done it this time, doggie, you've really done it!"

He lunged forward and I'm sorry to report that he got the tail. He didn't bite it off but he took a big chomp, jerked me off the ground, shook me like a stuffed toy, and flung me halfway across the street. Did it hurt? You bet it did, hurt like crazy, but guess what else happened.

In the process of trying to bite off my tail, *he jerked the steer into the trailer*! Deputy Kile raced to the trailer gate and slammed it shut, and suddenly we had achieved an enormous victory for the ranch, and shucks, for cowboys and dogs all across America.

For a long moment no one spoke. People on the street broke into applause. Deputy Kile gasped for breath and muttered, "I'm too old for this." Slim seemed to be in shock, but managed to say, "Good honk!"

Viola clapped her gloved hands together and shouted, "We did it! Good dog, Hank, good dog!"

Even though my tail throbbed, even though it had been bent into an odd shape, I rushed past the horse (he was grinning like a monkey) and leaped into her arms. Hearing her say "good dog" was all the reward I needed. The tail would straighten itself out in a week or two.

Everything was wonderful, but then...uh oh. Remember that incident at the Dixie Dog, the one involving a dog, a hamburger, and an angry lady? She had threatened to call you-know-who, and guess who came walking up in the midst of our victory celebration: Jimmy Joe Dogcatcher. The angry lady was with him.

Jimmy Joe and I had, uh, met on several occasions.

He pointed a finger at me. "Is that him?"

She glared at me with pinched eyes and pinched lips. "Yes sir, that's the one. He stole my Big Beefy and ran off with it."

Slim had climbed off his horse by then and joined us. Jimmy Joe looked him up and down. "Is this your dog?"

"I admit it, yes sir."

Jimmy Joe turned to the lady. "How much did they charge for the burger?"

"Well, it was double-meat and double-cheese. $4.95."

Jimmy Joe turned back to Slim. "You owe the lady five bucks. Your dog stole her burger."

"Would you take a check?"

"Not from you."

"I didn't bring my wallet."

"Well, life is tough."

Dead silence fell over us. The dogcatcher's mouth grew as tight and thin as barbed wire, and things were looking bad. Then...Deputy Kile heaved a sigh, dug out his wallet, and handed the lady a ten-dollar bill. "Here, ma'am, sorry for the inconvenience. I'll settle up with Slim."

Wow. I had a feeling that nobody but Deputy Kile could have pulled this off. See, if he hadn't been an officer of the law, Jimmy Joe might have thrown me into his cage and hauled me off to Devil's Island For Dogs, and that would have really messed up my life.

Jimmy Joe grunted something about cowboys and dogs, and went back to his pickup with the cage in the back.

The lady shook a finger at me and said, "Shame on you!" And she left too.

Slim took a big breath of air and looked down at me. "You don't stay a hero for long, pooch, but we got the job done." He turned to Deputy Kile. "Bobby, I take back all the bad things I've said about you over the years. Thanks, and you *will* get the ten bucks."

The deputy was looking rather stern and chewed his lip. "You didn't bring your wallet? I guess that means you're driving without a license. Judge McKinley won't like that."

Slim flinched. "Now, Bobby…"

"Get out of town, and next time, bring your wallet." He patted me on the head. "Nice job, Hank. You make Slim look almost like a real cowboy." He turned to Viola. "Thanks for the help and tell your folks hello."

Whew! Well, we had dodged a cannon ball, but we still had things to do. Slim moved the red steer into the front compartment with the other calves and led his horse to the trailer. I expected to hear another smart remark from Snips, but was astonished when he said, "That was pretty clever, dog. Thanks." He jumped into the trailer and Slim closed the gate.

What do you say when a horse gives you a compliment? It had never happened before. I was speechless.

Slim asked Viola if she would follow him out to the Bryan place east of town. She said of course. I jumped into Viola's pickup and we made our way out of town on a very slick highway.

At the Bryan place, Slim opened the wire gate, drove out into the field, and turned out the calves. Then he tested the electric fence (it was dead) and found the problem: three big tumbleweeds had shorted out the electricity.

He fixed the problem and turned to Viola. "With all this ice, I'd better leave my rig here. Loper and I can come get it when the ice melts. I'd hate to stack it at the bottom of that big hill going into the valley. Reckon I could hitch a ride home with you?"

She gave him a cute smile. "Oh, maybe, if you'll promise to take me to the dance at Lipscomb in May."

He swallowed hard. "Yes ma'm. I'm putty in your hands."

He unsaddled Snips and left him in the corral with hay and grain, then we all loaded into Viola's pickup and headed back to the ranch. It was a slow, slippery drive, and we're talking about thirty-five miles an hour. We stayed in four-wheel drive all the way.

I'm proud to report that I rode with my head in Viola's lap and several times, she rubbed my ears.

We inched our way down that big hill into the Wolf Creek valley and Viola kept both hands on the steering wheel, but we made it to the bottom and she relaxed a little bit. She looked at Slim. "Tell me the truth. Were you scared?"

"Roping a yearling on ice in the middle of

town? Nah, it was just another cowboy day."

"Honestly?"

"I was scared silly, but it had to be done." He glanced at me and grinned. "Hey, I just thought of a song about how this day started out. You want to hear it?"

"Of course!"

If he had asked me, I would have said, "Oh no! Please, not another of your corny songs!" See, I had a feeling that it would contain sensitive material about, well, about me. And I was right, but he didn't ask my opinion and he sang the tiresome thing. I was locked in the cab of the pickup and had to listen.

I don't suppose you'd want to hear it. You would? Okay, hang on.

Another Cowboy Day 2

This morning at seven, I flew out of bed.
The dogs were alarmed and my bedroom was red.
I reckon they thought that the house was on fire
And we were fixing to get ourselves broiled or fried.

I ran to the door, still half in a doze.
It was only the sunrise, as red as a rose.
The house wasn't burning and what can you say?

It's another cowboy day.

It's another cowboy day,
Checking the cattle and feeding 'em hay.
It's another cowboy day,
Just another cowboy day.

I looked for the camera all over my camp
But tripped over Hankie and busted the lamp.
When I opened the closet, an avalanche fell.
I should have known better than that, but oh well.

I grabbed up the camera and rushed to the porch
To capture that sunrise, as red as a torch.
But when I got there, the sky had turned gray.
Just another cowboy day.

Chorus

While I was so busy with my little part,
Old Hank was inventing a new kind of art.
Instead of just sleeping or chasing a mouse,
He strung toilet paper all over my house.

I have to admit I was tempted to curse,
I didn't suppose it could get any worse
Then Loper showed up and what could I say?

It's another cowboy day.

Chorus

Well, there it is. What did you think? I guess it wasn't too bad, but notice that he didn't mention that unrolling the T.P. had been *Drover's idea*.

Oh well, Viola thought it was a cute song and got a good laugh out of it. "That actually happened this morning?"

"Yes ma'am, honest."

Her smile faded and she took a slow, deep breath. "Slim, you must...stop...calling...me... MA'AM! My mother is 'ma'am.' My grandmother was 'ma'am.' The elderly ladies at church are 'ma'am.'"

"You're as cute as a button when you get mad."

"How would you like to walk back to the ranch?"

"You wouldn't do that." She pulled off the road and stopped. Slim was surprised. "It's five miles to headquarters."

"Education comes harder to some than to others."

"It's icy."

"Boo hoo."

He swallowed hard. "Yes, Viola, message received."

She looked down at me. "He's very stubborn, isn't he?"

Oh yes, worse than a donkey. I knew all about that.

Viola didn't make him walk home and Slim didn't call her 'ma'am' any more.

We made our way down the slippery Wolf Creek road and when we reached headquarters, we met Loper and Sally May and the kids in the flatbed pickup. They were just coming back from their feed run, putting out hay in all the pastures.

Loper was surprised to see us in Viola's pickup. "Okay, what happened?"

Slim explained that one of the steers escaped, ran into town, and destroyed Foxie's Lady's Wear. The police impounded the pickup and trailer, and were going to sell the cattle to pay for the damage.

"You're supposed to be in district court Monday morning. I gave 'em a full confession and told 'em what a skunk you are. Deputy Kile thinks they'll send you so far up the river, they'll have to pack your oxygen in on mules. The good news is that we get to keep the dog."

Sally May exploded in laughter (what was that supposed to mean?), but Loper remained stone-faced. He sighed and drummed the steering wheel with his fingers. "Viola, what happened?"

Viola was incapable of telling a lie, and she gave him the straight story. She ended by saying, "Slim was just..." She looked at him with eyes that sparkled. "He was just wonderful!"

Loper grunted. "Well, the important thing is that he didn't wreck my pickup. Get in, Mister Wonderful, we've still got chores to do."

Ah, the sadness! We said goodbye to Viola. Slim gave her a hug and thanked her for the help and the ride home. She engulfed me in her arms and cried and said she would miss me twice as much as she would miss Slim, and then she left with tears streaming down her cheeks.

Okay, maybe that's an exaggeration, but she was sad to leave me, no kidding.

And that's about the end of *The Frozen Rodeo*. It had been just another cowboy day, and...

This

      case

            is

                  closed.

Have you read all
of Hank's adventures?

And, be sure to check out the
Audiobooks!

If you've never heard a *Hank the Cowdog* audiobook, you're missing out on a lot of fun! Each Hank book has also been recorded as an unabridged audiobook for the whole family to enjoy!

Praise for the Hank Audiobooks:

"It's about time the Lone Star State stopped hogging Hank the Cowdog, the hilarious adventure series about a crime solving ranch dog. Ostensibly for children, the audio renditions by author John R. Erickson are sure to build a cult following among adults as well."   — *Parade Magazine*

"Full of regional humor . . . vocals are suitably poignant and ridiculous. A wonderful yarn."   — *Booklist*

"For the detectin' and protectin' exploits of the canine Mike Hammer, hang Hank's name right up there with those of other anthropomorphic greats...But there's no sentimentality in Hank: he's just plain more rip-roaring fun than the others. Hank's misadventures as head of ranch security on a spread somewhere in the Texas Panhandle are marvelous situation comedy."   — *School Library Journal*

"Knee-slapping funny and gets kids reading."

— *Fort Worth Star Telegram*

The Ranch Life Learning Series

Want to learn more about ranching? Check out Hank's hilarious and educational new series, Ranch Life Learning, brought to you by Maverick Books and The National Ranching Heritage Center!

Saddle up for some fun as the same cast of characters you've come to know and love in the Hank the Cowdog series gives you a first-class introduction to life on a ranch! In these books, you'll learn things like: the difference between a ranch and a farm, how cows digest grass, what it takes to run a ranch as a successful business, how to take care of cattle throughout the various seasons, what the daily life of a working cowboy looks like, qualities to look for in a good horse, the many kinds of wild animals you might see if you spent a few days on Hank's ranch, and much, much more!

And, coming in September 2020: *Ranch Weather*: Learn about the tremendous impact different kinds of weather have on every aspect of ranching!

Join Hank the Cowdog's Security Force

Are you a big Hank the Cowdog fan? Then you'll want to join Hank's Security Force. Here is some of the neat stuff you will receive:

Welcome Package
- A Hank paperback of your choice
- An original Hank poster (19" x 25")
- A Hank bookmark

Eight digital issues of *The Hank Times* newspaper with
- Lots of great games and puzzles
- Stories about Hank and his friends
- Special previews of future books
- Fun contests

More Security Force Benefits
- Special discounts on Hank books, audios, and more
- Special Members Only section on Hank's website at www.hankthecowdog.com

Total value of the Welcome Package and *The Hank Times* is $23.99. However, your two-year membership is **only $7.99** plus $5.00 for shipping and handling.

- -

☐ Yes, I want to join Hank's Security Force. Enclosed is $12.99 ($7.99 + $5.00 for shipping and handling) for my **two-year membership**. [Make check payable to Maverick Books. International shipping extra.]

WHICH BOOK WOULD YOU LIKE TO RECEIVE IN YOUR WELCOME PACKAGE?
CHOOSE ANY BOOK IN THE SERIES. (EXCEPT #50)   (#   )

_____

                                          BOY or GIRL
YOUR NAME   (CIRCLE ONE)
_____

MAILING ADDRESS
_____

CITY   STATE   ZIP
_____

TELEPHONE   BIRTH DATE
_____

E-MAIL (REQUIRED FOR DIGITAL HANK TIMES)

Send check or money order for $12.99 to:

Hank's Security Force
Maverick Books
P.O. Box 549
Perryton, Texas 79070
Offer is subject to change

DO NOT SEND CASH.   NO CREDIT CARDS ACCEPTED.
ALLOW 2-3 WEEKS FOR DELIVERY

The following activities are samples from *The Hank Times*, the official newspaper of Hank's Security Force. Please do not write on these pages unless this is your book. And, even then, why not just find a scrap of paper?

"Rhyme Time"

~~~~~~

What if Deputy Kile were to decide to give up his job as a police officer and go in search of other work? What kinds of jobs could he find?

Make a rhyme using "Kile" that would relate to his new job possibilities.

Example: Deputy KILE starts a company making these special sweaters.

Answer: Kile **ARGYLE.**

1. Deputy KILE gets a job helping people keep their papers organized.

2. Deputy KILE becomes a fashion designer.

G.L.Holmes

3. Deputy KILE teaches people how to be happy.

4. Deputy KILE retires to live on a piece of land surrounded by water.

5. Deputy KILE becomes a court judge.

6. Deputy KILE gets a job walking off and marking every 5,280 feet.

7. Deputy KILE delivers stacked bundles of firewood.

8. Deputy KILE installs this special kind of flooring.

Answers:

1. Kile FILE   3. Kile SMILE   5. Kile TRIAL   7. Kile PILE
2. Kile STYLE   4. Kile ISLE   6. Kile MILE   8. Kile TILE

"Word Maker"

Try making up to twenty words from the letters in the names below. Use as many letters as possible, however, don't just add an "s" to a word you've already listed in order to have it count as another. Try to make up entirely new words for each line!

Then, count the total number of letters used in all of the words you made, and see how well you did using the Security Force Rankings below!

DEPUTY   KILE

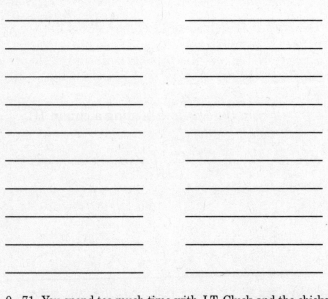

0 - 71 You spend too much time with J.T. Cluck and the chickens.

72 - 74 You are showing some real Security Force potential.

75 - 77 You have earned a spot on our Ranch Security team.

78 +   Wow! You rank up there as a top-of-the-line cowdog.

"Photogenic" Memory Quiz

We all know that Hank has a "photogenic" memory—being aware of your surroundings is an important quality for a Head of Ranch Security. Now *you* can test your powers of observation.

How good is your memory? Look at the illustration on the cover and try to remember as many things about it as possible. Then turn back to this page and see how many questions you can answer.

1. What color is the lady's coat?
   Green, Grey, Purple, or Brown?

2. Is the guy in the window holding a cup in HIS Left or Right hand?

3. What color shirt was the guy at the door wearing? Purple, Green, or Blue?

4. Was the cup in the air tilted Up or Down?

5. What color were the letters in DIXIE DOG? Gold, Silver, or Green?

6. How many of Hank's eyes could you see? 1, 2 or all 4?

Have you visited Hank's official website yet?

www.hankthecowdog.com

Don't miss out on exciting *Hank the Cowdog* games and activities, as well as up-to-date news about upcoming books in the series!

When you visit, you'll find:

- Hank's BLOG, which is the first place we announce upcoming books and new products!
- Hank's Official Shop, with tons of great *Hank the Cowdog* books, audiobooks, games, t-shirts, stuffed animals, mugs, bags, and more!
- Links to Hank's social media, whereby Hank sends out his "Cowdog Wisdom" to fans.
- A FREE, printable "Map of Hank's Ranch"!
- Hank's Music Page where you can listen to songs and even download FREE ringtones!
- A way to sign up for Hank's free email updates
- Sally May's "Ranch Roundup Recipes"!
- Printable & Colorable Greeting Cards for Holidays.
- Articles about Hank and author John R. Erickson in the news,

...AND MUCH, MUCH MORE!

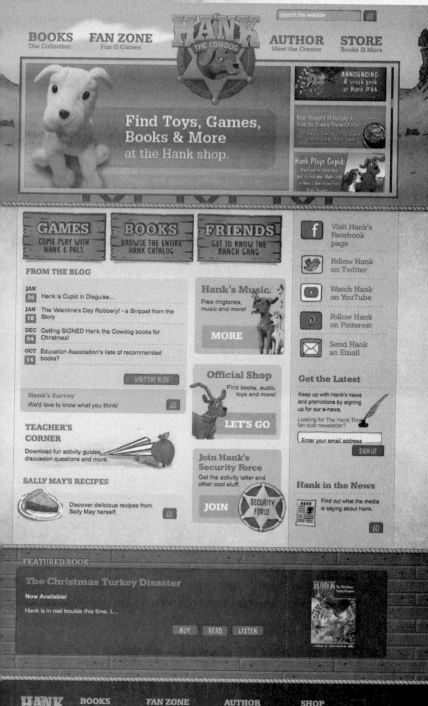

Love Hank's Hilarious Songs?

Hank the Cowdog's "Greatest Hits" albums bring together the music from the unabridged audiobooks you know and love! These wonderful collections of hilarious (and sometimes touching) songs are unmatched. Where else can you learn about coyote philosophy, buzzard lore, why your dog is protecting an old corncob, how bugs compare to hot dog buns, and much more!

And, be sure to visit Hank's "Music Page" on the official website to listen to some of the songs and download FREE Hank the Cowdog ringtones!

"Audio-Only" Stories

Ever wondered what those "Audio-Only" Stories in Hank's Official Store are all about?

The Audio-Only Stories are Hank the Cowdog adventures that have never been released as books. They are about half the length of a typical Hank book, and there are currently seven of them. They have run as serial stories in newspapers for years and are now available as audiobooks!

Photo Courtesy of Western Horseman Magazine

John R. Erickson,

a former cowboy, has written numerous books for both children and adults and is best known for his acclaimed *Hank the Cowdog* series. The *Hank* series began as a self-publishing venture in Erickson's garage in 1982 and has endured to become one of the nation's most popular series for children and families.

Through the eyes of Hank the Cowdog, a smelly, smart-aleck Head of Ranch Security, Erickson gives readers a glimpse into daily life on a cattle ranch in the West Texas Panhandle. His stories have won a number of awards, including the Audie, Oppenheimer, Wrangler, and Lamplighter Awards, and have been translated into Spanish, Danish, Farsi, and Chinese. *USA Today* calls the *Hank the Cowdog* books "the best family entertainment in years." Erickson lives and works on his ranch in Perryton, Texas, with his family.

Gerald L. Holmes

was a largely self-taught artist who grew up on a ranch in Oklahoma. For over thirty-seven years, he illustrated the *Hank the Cowdog* books and serial stories, as well as numerous other cartoons and textbooks, and his paintings have been featured in various galleries across the United States. He and his wife lived in Perryton, Texas, where they raised their family.

Shawn Tevis Photography